Chasing Victory: A Romantic Comedy

The Dartmouth Diaries Book Four

Beverley Watts

BaR Publishing

Contents

Author's Note

You may have noticed that I've used quite a lot of naval colloquialisms throughout The Dartmouth Diaries – most of which I believe are generally understandable in context (I hope so anyway!)

However, in Chasing Victory I mention the word Pompey. For the benefit of all non naval personnel (which is most of you I suspect), Pompey is an affectionate nick name for the city of Portsmouth on the south coast of England - still regarded by many as the sacred home of the Royal Navy.

Also, just in case you're interested, nearly all of the colloquialisms I've used throughout the series have been purloined from *Jack Speak* by Rick Jolly - a comprehensive guide to the humorous and colourful slang of Britain's senior service.

I have spent many a happy hour chuckling away at some of the more *lively* phrases!

You can order a copy by visiting the link below:

Jackspeak-guide-British-Naval-slang

Chapter One

'Those are salad tongs, you are NOT putting any bloody kitchenware in there.'

Victory Westbrook, my best friend since forever, is in labour. Nearly three weeks early. And her husband of six months, the totally gorgeous, more famous than the Queen, Oscar nominated actor Noah Westbrook, is stuck in an airport in Canada. Fog bound. In June. Which means I get to be her birthing partner instead...

Wincing sympathetically, I lean forward to wipe Tory's sweating brow. 'Sweetie, you need some help getting junior out. It's been over ten hours and you're knackered.'

Tory moans in answer, and grabs hold of the gas and air. 'I feel like bloody Darth Vadar,' she mutters, plastering the mouthpiece to her face. After taking a deep breath in, she glares at the doctor before saying in a slightly slurry voice, 'Okay, do your worst. Maybe you can check out my tonsils while you're in there.'

Ten minutes later Isaac Charles Westbrook arrives into the world kicking and screaming, a whopping nine pound four.

'Oh my God Tory he's beautiful,' I murmur as the midwife places the little red bundle onto her chest.

'He is, isn't he,' she responds tearfully, stroking his head gently.

As I stare down at mother and baby, I feel the sudden unfamiliar stirrings of envy. I've never considered myself parent material. I've always been pretty blasé about it – if it happened, it happened, sort of thing. The world is vastly overpopulated anyway. But standing there looking at my best friend - weary, but literally glowing with happiness, I feel my maternal instinct kick in with all the force of a charging rhino.

Swallowing a sudden lump in my throat the size of a golf ball, I lean forward and hug them both, breathing in the scent of new baby, helplessly wondering where Jason stands in regards to siring a couple of little Buchannans in the not too distant future.

Although we've been dating since Tory and Noah's wedding last December, and things have been pretty good, we haven't really gotten around to discussing the important life changing stuff like children. To be fair, Jason's job means that we don't get an awful lot of time together – although I have been wheeled out of the closet as his significant other at various naval functions.

Jason Buchannan is a captain in the Royal Navy, and currently he's the Captain of Britannia Royal Naval College - the RN's premier officer training establishment, situated high on a hill overlooking the picturesque yachting town of Dartmouth in the south west of England. It's all very queen and country with a liberal dose of stiff upper lip. Jason suits it like he was born to it. Me? Not so much. But hey, so far I haven't managed to cause a diplomatic incident...

Forcing my mind back to the matter at hand, I follow the orderlies as they wheel Tory's bed up to the maternity ward. As Noah Westbrook's wife, she could have had specialist treatment in a private clinic, but she insisted on having her baby at the local hospital in Torquay and giving them a donation equal to the cost of private care. No idea why, just one of Tory's quirks.

Once she's settled in, I give both her and Isaac a last kiss before heading out to my car. I have a list of items Tory all of a sudden deems necessary for her stay in hospital – although why she thinks a tin opener is likely to be useful is anybody's guess. But if I do the fetching and carrying, Noah gets to head straight to the hospital when he finally arrives. The last text said he he'd just landed in Heathrow.

It takes me twenty minutes to get from Torquay to the Higher Car Ferry. Dartmouth sits at the mouth of the River Dart, so getting to it from the holiday resort of Torbay necessitates crossing the river. All well and good most of the time, but a hell of a challenge at stupid o'clock in the morning. However, Tory's father lives this side of the river, so I have a small detour to make before I cross over.

Turning into a small road, just before the last few yards to the river's edge, I finally pull up outside a massive fence and gate which would do justice to Buckingham Palace.

Tory's dad is affectionately known locally as the Admiral – for the obvious reason that he was an Admiral in the Royal Navy. I say affectionately. There are those who would just as soon ring his neck given the penchant he has for meddling in affairs that are none of his business. But then, knowing him is never ever dull. Goodness knows how little Isaac will fare, having him as a role model...

Climbing out of the car, I press the buzzer next to the gate and settle back to wait. Both gate and fence came courtesy of *The Bridegroom* – a romantic comedy which was a massive box office success two years ago. Part of the movie was filmed at the Admiral's house - a large Edwardian pile with the rather original name of the Admiralty. Tory was living at home at the time. Noah was the leading man and voila – the rest as they say is history.

'You can tell your bollocking editor that I've got nothing to say apart from take your bloody pen and paper and shove it up your duck run.' The Admiral's voice booms out of the small intercom, and instinctively I glance up and step back. Tory's father obviously thinks I'm some kind of undesirable and he's been known to discourage such unwanted visitors by lobbing something unpleasant over the fence. Although to be fair, that little inclination only surfaced to dissuade the more determined paparazzi camping outside his back door once Tory and Noah became an item.

'Admiral it's me, Kit,' I yell back hastily, concerned he might turn off the intercom and that would be that. I'd have a better chance of getting in to Fort Knox. I can hear Dotty and Pickles barking frenziedly in the background, drawing an answering mutter of, 'What a bloody cake and arse party.' Then without warning he changes volume and his voice blasts directly into the intercom, giving me a mini heart attack.

'PIPE DOWN YOU MISERABLE MUTTS OR YOU'LL BOTH BE RELEGATED TO THE BOLLOCKING SHED FOR THE REST OF YOUR BLOODY NATURAL.'

I take a deep breath, heart still pounding, getting ready to add my own contribution to the din, but luckily before I get chance to join in, the buzzer goes off and the gate clicks open. Murmuring a quick prayer of thanks, I hurry through to give Tory's father the good news.

Half an hour later I'm pulling off the car ferry on the Dartmouth side of the river. I can't help but smile to myself as I remember the Admiral's delight when I told him he had a grandson. He insisted on pouring us both a glass of Port to toast his first carpet crawler. When I showed him a couple of photos I'd taken on my phone, he pronounced with satisfaction that Isaac was definitely Victory's as he had the Shackleford chin. I didn't like to ask who else's he thought the baby could be...

After parking my car in the garage, I make a quick phone call to Freddy to appraise him that he's become an honorary uncle, and his squeal of excitement is in complete contrast to his earlier blasé attitude towards Tory's pregnancy. Our gay friend wastes no time in vowing to ensure that little Isaac doesn't lose touch with his feminine side which I'm not sure is necessarily a good thing, and agreeing to meet me and the Admiral at the hospital as soon as he's finished at work. Cutting the call, I pop quickly up to my flat to have a shower and get changed.

Tory showed the first signs of labour at four o'clock yesterday afternoon, so I dashed over to her house with nothing but the clothes I was standing up in, envisioning myself rushing her to the hospital in a car journey straight out of the movie *Fast and Furious*. However, I don't think they ever filmed *Fast and Furious* during a seaside town's rush hour - it took us so long to get to the hospital, Tory could have delivered triplets. It was a good job her waters didn't actually break until two in the morning.

This time, determined to avoid a repeat performance of *Slow and Laborious*, I'm back outside the Admiralty by three in the afternoon, before the local schools begin regurgitating their pupils. As Tory's father squeezes himself into my ten year old Fiesta, I briefly mourn the loss of my beloved seven seater, sacrificed nearly a year ago on the altar of unemployment. Although things have definitely been looking up since I organized my best friend's high profile wedding last December, I've nevertheless not quite reached the dizzy heights of corporate cardom.

The Admiral is uncharacteristically silent as we head over to the hospital. It actually feels quite strange being in an enclosed space with Tory's dad, especially after the revelation that he and my Aunt Flo had once been married.

'Is Dotty behaving herself?' I ask finally as the silence becomes a little oppressive

The Admiral frowns at me before offering the word, 'Spoilt,' along with a humph that makes his feelings about the little dog perfectly clear. I can't help but wince a little. Being looked after by the Admiral must be akin to going from a five star hotel to a zero star hostel. Still, at least she's got Pickles.

'You spoken to your aunt yet?' The Admiral's question takes me completely by surprise and I cast him a wary glance while frantically thinking what to say.

'I take it that means no,' he continues gruffly when I take too long. 'You can't ignore it forever Kit Davies, the whole bollocking load of horlicks has been under wraps for far too bloody long. It's time to get it all out in the open.'

I throw another, this time incredulous, glance at the man whose penchant for secrets is pretty much legendary, and he has the grace to look a little embarrassed before determinedly ploughing ahead, his voice at once defiant and sincere. 'The thing is Kit, secrets have a way of catching up with you when you least want them to, and let's be honest, I should bloody well know.'

The truth is, I haven't spoken to my aunt about my less than

conventional entrance to this world. Despite my initial deter-
mination to know the whole sordid truth, there's a big part of
me that enjoys being in cloud cuckoo land about the whole affair.
Surely it's enough to know that my father was a complete nut-
case and I'm lucky Aunt Flo managed to sneak me away from his
corrupt influence and bring me back to the UK - after blowing
his brains out of course.

Surely that's enough?

Coughing awkwardly, I concentrate on pulling out of a junc-
tion into the heavy oncoming traffic. Jason, Tory and Freddy
have been badgering me for months to have The Conversation
with my aunt. In fact the only two people on the planet who
seem reluctant to have this particular tête-à-tête are me and
Aunt Flo. Oh things are okay between us, and if we haven't quite
got back to the familiar, easy relationship we had before she
dropped her bombshell, well no-one would know it apart from
the two of us. I think we're just happy to let sleeping dogs lie. Or
maybe I just can't bring myself to ask her why she abandoned me
in Dartmouth as a scared two year old because I don't think I'm
going to like the answer.

Determinedly I turn my mind back to my driving, promising
myself that I'll speak to Aunt Flo – soon...

Six hours later, Freddy and I are wetting little Isaac's head in
The Cherub, and it has to be said that all the excitement has
definitely gone to our heads – or it might be the two bottles of
Prosecco we've just consumed.

'I'm going to be the best uncle since *Uncle Buck*.' Freddy's words
are definitely slightly slurred.

'I thought he was supposed to be a totally crap uncle in that
movie.'

'Nope. He was awesome. Got on the same level as the kids, totally rocked it. That's gonna be me.'

'You're going to have to put some weight on then if you're
going to measure up to John Candy.'

Freddy frowns at my drunken observation, looking down at

himself in dismay. 'You're right,' he murmurs, 'Damn, I'd better order some chips.'

'The grease will definitely soak up the alcohol.' Noah's voice is wry, which of course is completely lost on both of us and I jump up with a very unlady like squeal, throwing my arms around my best friend's husband in an enthusiastic rugby tackle. Staggering under my unreserved hug, Noah laughs, holding me briefly before setting me carefully back on my feet.

'I'm not sure you guys are a good influence on my son,' he growls, his grin belying his stern words. 'I think it's gonna take more than a few fries to get you both sober, I'll order a couple of pizzas.

'Is Jason coming over?' Noah's last words throw a dash of cold water over my delightfully alcoholic haze, doing a better job of sobering me up than any amount of fast food.

'I'm not sure, I haven't managed to speak to him since yesterday. We've left each other a couple of messages, but so far we've been playing answer phone ping pong. I think he's been in meetings pretty much all day.' I omit the part where Jason's voice in his last message this afternoon sounded cold and distant, causing my heart to flutter uncomfortably. 'I'm sure he'll make it if he can,' I continue determinedly cheerful in the face of Noah's too perceptive glance. Luckily, he doesn't pursue it any further and heads to the bar.

'That's not like you and Jason. Thought you murmured sweet nothings to each other at least twenty times a day.' Freddy's light words do nothing to alleviate my anxiety and my response is sharper than I intended. 'I think you're referring to you and Jacques. Your phone bill must be the size of a small mortgage since he's been in America.'

'God, that's good.' Noah's arrival back from the bar with his pint effectively puts an end to the conversation and I gratefully turn the subject back to baby talk.

'How are Tory and little Isaac,' I ask, delighting in the look of pride and joy that immediately transforms his face.

'Well, aside from my wife being the most amazing woman on

both sides of the Atlantic, and my son obviously the most beautiful baby ever to be born, I'm pleased to report that both are doing fantastic. I should be able to pick them up tomorrow morning after the pediatrician's stopped by.

'I can't thank you enough for being there with her Kit, I was going crazy stuck in Toronto.' The relief in his voice that everything turned out okay is palpable and I put my hand over his with a smile.

'Hey, that's what friends are for. And anyway, it was very enlightening – and not just for whole getting to see a baby born thing, which of course was absolutely awesome – I actually think Tory used her father's entire repertoire of swear words. You should have seen the midwife's face.'

Noah laughs again, effectively ending the gravity of the moment. 'Hopefully I'll get to see it next time.'

Then he looks around the small bar at the cluster of regulars who are trying very hard not to eavesdrop, and stands up with a grin. 'I'm not sure if you guys know it, but I've become a father today. Go grab whatever your poison is, the drinks are on me.' His words prompt a smattering of applause followed by lots of back patting, not to mention parental advice. I have time to wince at an old wives remedy for colic, when my phone rings. Glancing down, my stomach does a slight skip as Jason's name flashes across the screen.

'Hey you, had a busy day?' For some reason my voice comes out hoarse and dry.

'Sorry I didn't get back to you earlier.' His voice is clipped and short, a tone I haven't heard from him in months, and my heart slams against my ribs in an instinctive response.

'What's wrong?' I ask automatically, unable to stem the rising tide of fear in my gut.

He sighs, and for a second I think I've imagined everything, then he continues, 'It's my father Kit. He's had a stroke. I'm on my way up to Scotland now.'

Chapter Two

I t's two in the morning and I'm lying in bed unable to sleep. The pizza is sitting in my stomach like it was made of concrete, and my mind is going over and over my last conversation with Jason.

It seems he's been aware of his father's deteriorating health for a couple of weeks, so apparently the stroke didn't come as a complete surprise. Except to me.

I wanted to ask him why he hadn't shared his concerns with me, why after six months he didn't feel he could unburden himself, reveal his worries. But the words stuck in my throat, and instead I responded to his impersonal tone in the same monosyllabic voice, not knowing how to comfort him, or what to say to make things better. In the end, when we finished the call, my first thought was that I'd lost him.

He said he'd call me when he got to Glasgow. I glance at the clock. He won't be there yet, even if he drives well over the speed limit. I think back over the last few weeks. How come I'm only now realizing that Jason has been uncharacteristically withdrawn? Have I been so wrapped up with my burgeoning business and Tory's pregnancy that I haven't noticed? What does that say about our relationship, and more importantly, what does it say about me?

I spend the rest of the night tossing and turning, in between staring at the clock and checking my mobile phone. At five thirty, I give in and get up to make myself a cup of tea. Just as I take the first sip, my phone finally rings.

'Hey babe, you okay? How's your dad?' My voice when I answer is breathless, matching the samba my heart is doing against my ribs. To my relief, his response is much more upbeat than our last conversation. 'He's doing okay. Luckily it was only a minor stroke – more of a warning really. When I left him he was sitting up in bed flirting with one of the nurses.'

'Thank God,' I answer with an enthusiasm I don't have to force. Jason's father Hugo is a sweet man and I've genuinely come to care for him.

'He'll be in hospital for a week or so while they run some tests,' Jason continues, 'Then he'll need some kind of nursing care back at the Tower until he's completely back on his feet. I'm just about to drive back to Dartmouth to attend the dinner tonight, then I'll head back up here this weekend.'

The dinner, the bloody bollocking dinner. I'd forgotten all about it. Shit, shit, shit…

'You haven't forgotten that we're entertaining the new First Sea Lord this evening have you?' His voice is now slightly exasperated. Maybe he knows me better than I think. 'Of course not sweetheart, why would you think that?'

'Why indeed?' is his dry response. 'Can you be up at the house for about eighteen thirty? We'll be having pre-dinner drinks on the terrace at nineteen hundred.'

I promise faithfully to be there, my mind already frantically converting the bloody military timing to the bog standard way the rest of us mortals refer to time, as well as cataloguing everything I have to do today: Two new prospective clients, the final preparations for a wedding on Saturday and a funeral on Monday. And I haven't bought anything to wear yet. Bugger, I'd better get started…

I've had the day from hell. This evening can only be an improvement. There's been a mistake made in the order of service leaflets for Mr Alexander Smeelie's funeral service - there's a lovely picture of the gentleman in question on the front with the words Alexander Smellie.

And the favours ordered for Saturday's wedding are mini penises. I think they've got them confused with a hen party.

By the time I dash into Dartmouth's most up market boutique for a little black number that shouts sexy sophistication, it's already four forty five. I frantically search through the dozen long black dresses (Jason was pretty specific over what I should wear – maybe he should have bloody well bought me one), and quickly decide on a jersey number that I think fits the bill. No time to try it on, but I'm a pretty standard size ten, so I hand over my credit card with a prayer that there's still enough left on it.

After laying my appallingly expensive purchase on the bed, I grab a quick shower and put on my makeup. Luckily my hair is still doing the short pixie thing so needs very little attention. I glance at my watch – five forty five, just enough time for a fortifying glass of wine before I need to get dressed.

With a sigh of relief, I take a large sip of my Pinot Blush and sit down on my bed, stroking the fabric of my new dress with my free hand. It really was horrendously expensive - I hope Jason bloody well appreciates it. Then I stifle a giggle. As my beloved is sending a car down for me, I can go ahead and wear my killer black heels. And I know for a fact that he appreciates those…

All of a sudden I'm looking forward to the evening. Jason wants me there as his partner and I'm determined to make him proud of me. Swallowing back the rest of the wine, I put the glass on the side and pick up the silky length of material. Trying to figure out the best way to put it on, I finally allow it to pool on the floor and step into the hole. The fabric is smooth and clingy. There's no way I'll be able to wear any underwear. I'm actually getting a little turned on by the thought that Jason will know I'm wearing nothing underneath. Now if that's not sexy sophistication, I don't know what is.

I pull the sleeves over each arm and frown slightly. The dress obviously dips at the back. But that's okay, this is one of those times where having small pert boobs actually works in my favour. The front neckline has a slight cowl in it, so I turn towards the full length mirror on the closet to make sure it's sitting cor-

CHASING VICTORY: A ROMANTIC COMEDY

rectly. The dress fits me like a glove, the length perfect.

As I stare in delight, congratulating myself on my superior dress sense, I hear a car horn beep outside the flat window, signalling my lift is here. Grabbing my purse and wrap, I hurry down the steep stairs to the street.

Five minutes later we're in the College grounds, winding our way up the hill to Jason's house. The Naval College is a magnificent red brick building constructed at the turn of the century, and as Captain of said College, Jason gets to live in the imposing mansion tagged on to the side of it. I always have to fight the urge to curtsy to him when I'm in there. Needless to say we haven't done the deed on any of the drawing room sofas...

After thanking the driver, I step out of the car, wincing a little at the draft on my back. Hurriedly I settle the wrap over my ensemble and head to the front door where Dave the butler (apparently he's not a butler, he's a steward, but he definitely looks like a butler to me) is waiting.

'Hi Dave,' I smile, handing him my wrap. 'Is Captain Buchannan in the drawing room?'

'Yes ma'am. He asks that you go right in.' Looking forward to Jason's gasp of admiration, I sweep towards the drawing room door, only faltering slightly as I hear Dave's sudden indrawn breath behind me. Bless, it's good to know that I can still affect members of the opposite sex, even if I'm no longer quite the nubile young thing I was in my twenties.

Reaching the door, I pause for effect and as Jason turns towards me, I shiver at his intense silver gaze. His eyes travel the full length of my body and the heat in them shouts his approval. 'Would you like a drink?' he asks finally, his voice gratifyingly hoarse. I nod my head with a wide smile and sashay towards him, only stopping when there are inches between us and he can smell my perfume and feel the heat of my body. He bends his head to kiss my neck, and I lean my own head to one side to give him better access, holding my breath in anticipation.

But instead of the anticipated feel of his lips, he stiffens and stops completely still. Then, before I can ask if something's

13

wrong, he grasps my shoulders and spins me round. 'Hey,' I squeal in surprise, 'What...?'

'...The hell are you wearing,' he finishes, his voice low and furious. I frown in indignation at his tone, trying to turn back round. What the hell's the matter with the bloody man? Surely he can't object to a simple black dress.

Before I get chance to speak however, he ignores my spluttering and marches me towards a long mirror on the other side of the room. Once in front of the glass, he brusquely turns me to the side, exposing my back. My naked back. My very, very naked back, all the way to my very, very naked bottom...

My protests die as I stare at my reflection in horrified silence.

'What are you trying to do?' he finally grinds out, 'Help get me promoted the old fashioned way?'

'I didn't know,' I protest faintly, 'I...I didn't have time to try the dress on. I had no idea it was... quite so revealing at the back.'

'That's putting it mildly,' is his unrelenting response. Mortified, I glance up at his face, as he runs his hand distractedly through his hair, the gesture showing more than anything what an unforgivable gaff I've made. Stepping forward he propels me towards another door, like a child about to be scolded. Lost in misery, I allow him to pull me into the large old fashioned kitchen where several eyes swivel towards us – away from Dave who had obviously been regaling the entire kitchen staff about the inappropriateness of my attire.

'Mrs. McCaffrey, do you have a sewing kit on hand?'

The elderly cook proves to be a dab hand with a needle and thread and potential disaster is averted. I'm back in the drawing room only a few minutes after the First Sea Lord, aka Admiral Sir Philip James and his entourage arrive, and firmly putting aside the horrifying vision of what might have been, I set out to prove that I really do have the necessary grace and refinement to be a significant asset to Jason's naval career, (and not in the old fashioned way...)

Consequently dinner is a resounding success. Sir Philip is totally enamoured with my witty comebacks and sophisticated banter, and I can see Jason visibly relaxing at the other side of the table. I feel giddy with triumph. This is me at my sparkling, charming best. Who knew I had such hidden talents?

As we finish dessert, Jason suggests that we take coffee and Port back in the drawing room and nodding gracefully, I slide back my chair with poise and confidence. That is until my hem gets caught up under the back leg, and as I try to free it, the neatly sewn back of my dress slowly unravels.

Yanking viciously at the offending fabric, I straighten up quickly, glancing around to see if anyone has noticed, but fortunately my back is to the wall. For a split second I panic, what the hell am I going to do? If Sir Philip gets an eyeful of my bottom, every bit of effort I've put it to this evening will go down the Swannee. I might as well just ask if he's brought any condoms. Gnawing on my bottom lip, I wonder if anyone would notice if I just stayed here.

'Darling, could you come over and pour?' Jason's voice is light and relaxed. I feel sick.

'Coming sweetheart,' I respond after a few seconds, hoping my voice doesn't sound too much like Alvin The Chipmunk. Carefully I walk over to the dining room door, pausing slightly, my eyes scanning the room and its occupants in a move that would have impressed Marta Hari. In a few short seconds I note that nearly everyone is sitting on the sofas and chairs grouped around the coffee table. That is everyone bar one. Captain Whatever his name is, is currently admiring the view from the French Windows.

There's only one route open to me to ensure that nobody cops an intimate view of my nether regions. Adopting a serene smile that would have given Mother Theresa a run for her money, I attempt a nonchalant sideways saunter, swaying slightly like I have an irresistible tune in my head. As I catch a glimpse of myself in the same mirror that revealed my original faux pas, I realize that to anyone catching a glimpse it looks as though I'm bloody line dancing. Luckily everyone is busy helping themselves to Port. I can feel the sweat begin to tickle my back as I weave my way around the room with one eye on the group around the coffee table and the other on Captain What's his name, careful to keep my back hidden to both.

It takes me two excruciating minutes to finally approach the only empty chair, the one with the coffee pot and several cups placed conveniently in front of it. However, the last few yards will leave my behind exposed to Captain What's his face in a view that could well rival the one he's currently admiring.

Jason glances up at me with a smile. He's about to speak, I know he is. The minute he opens his mouth, Captain Who Je Me flip is going to turn round.

I panic. With a gay laugh which unfortunately comes out like a maniacal cackle, I launch myself at the chair as though I'm about to throw a rugby tackle. As I slide into it at top speed, I have to fight the urge to shout, 'Geronimo.' Everyone looks up in surprise. I bounce off the arm of the chair and land on the cushion with a resounding woomph and favour them all with a triumphant stare, just as the arm of my dress slides off one shoulder, completely exposing my right breast.

Chapter Three

'I'm so, so sorry Jason, I know you must be really angry, and of course you have every right, but... but, well I don't know what else to say.'

Our illustrious guests have gone, and Sir Philip, who is obviously staying the night, has retired to bed, leaving the two of us sitting alone in the drawing room with a night cap. Or in Jason's case, night caps in the plural. I'm not sure whether he's on his third or his fifth brandy. Good job I hate the stuff or I'd be matching him glass for glass.

I genuinely don't know what else to say. I just feel like crying. For the last five minutes, he's said absolutely nothing, just stared broodingly into his glass, until I have the horrible, terrible feeling he's about to break up with me. And I don't blame him. I would break up with me if I were in Jason's shoes. I couldn't have embarrassed him more if I'd stood on the coffee table and launched into a rounding rendition of *Hey Big Spender*.

I open my mouth to say sorry again, when he suddenly looks up. My heart thuds painfully at the seriousness of his gaze. 'Here it comes,' I think, mentally preparing myself for what he's about to say.

'I'm thinking of resigning my commission.' His voice is low and even. It's so not what I expected him to say and I look at him blankly until he sighs impatiently, and knocks back the rest of his brandy. 'I'm leaving the Navy,' he repeats in ordinary mortal speak.

'But, I thought you loved your job,' I whisper finally. 'Is this because of what happened tonight? I promise it won't happen again, I'll make sure that anything I wear is completely appropriate; I swear the next dress I wear will be a polo neck. You don't ha...'

Jason puts his finger gently over my lips, effectively silencing my rambling. His faint smile takes the sting out of his action, and when I stumble to a halt, he takes his hand away from my mouth and curls it into my neck. 'This isn't about tonight Kit. It's something I've been thinking about more and more often of late. My father isn't getting any younger and he's struggling to cope with Bloodstone Tower on his own. His stroke has simply brought home the fact that it's up to me to take the burden away from him.'

'But that will mean you leaving Dartmouth,' I protest, the knowledge landing like a blow in my chest.

'It won't be for another twelve months,' he responds calmly, 'And I was always going to leave Dartmouth anyway, you know that Kit. My draft here is only for two years, then I could well be given command of a ship.' I simply stare at him, wide eyed. 'I thought you knew that,' he continues quietly when I don't respond.

'I did... I do,' I stutter eventually, 'But I..I...thought...' I sputter to a halt, not knowing what the hell I thought. 'It's just that Scotland is such a long way away,' I finish eventually, lamely.

'Not as far as The Gulf,' is his dry response.

I don't answer, my stomach is churning. I hate change, I always have. Why deal with today what you can put off until tomorrow?

I take a large stinging gulp of my brandy, feeling the contents burn their way down, causing my throat to spasm violently. 'I've had a long distance relationship,' I whisper hoarsely after my coughing finally subsides, 'And in my experience it doesn't work.'

'I don't want a long distance relationship,' he answers, looking at me steadily, 'I want you to come up to Scotland with me.'

~*~

'What did you say to him?' Tory's voice is light but I can hear her underlying concern.

We're sitting in my flat each nursing a glass of wine. The early evening sun is streaming through the balcony windows, giving a warm glow to the room. Baby Isaac is snoring gently in his carry-cot and Dotty is snoozing on her lap. Everything is peaceful.

This is Tory's first glass of wine since becoming a new mother, and as it's the only one she's allowed while breast feeding, she's taking tiny minute sips. It will probably last for another three hours at this rate. Not like me unfortunately. I'm well into my second glass, still brooding after last night's little tête-à-tête.

'I didn't know what to say,' I respond glumly. 'I had no idea he was even thinking of coming out of the RN.'

'But surely you knew he wouldn't be at Dartmouth forever?' Tory's question echoes Jason's earlier comment and I realize just how naïve (could be translated as stupid) I've been.

'I never gave it any thought,' I mutter eventually as my best friend shakes her head in exasperation.

'To be fair, I've been focusing on my new event management business,' I continue pompously, indignation finally replacing the earlier self pity.

Taking another tiny sip of her wine, Tory closes her eyes in brief bliss before nodding her head a little more sympathetically. 'I know Kitty Kat, but you must admit you're even worse than me when it comes to burying your head in the sand.' I open my mouth to protest then close it again with a sigh. 'I know you're right,' I murmur resignedly, 'I just thought it would all work out somehow.'

'Well it has,' is Tory's matter of fact response, 'Just not in the way you might have wanted.' I give another sigh and reach for the bottle.

'Do you love Jason?' Tory's question is blunt, her tone almost aggressive, and I look up from the bottom of my glass in surprise. I open my mouth to say, 'Of course,' when the look in her eyes makes me pause. I realize she's not just asking an idle question. She really does want to know the answer, and her gaze is challenging me to think twice before I come out with anything flippant.

'That's easy for you to say,' I respond sharply, slightly stung by the challenge in her eyes, 'The man you fell in love with chose to settle half a world away from his home to be with you.'

Tory narrows her eyes slightly and for a second I think it's going to develop into a playground argument, but she opts for another sip of wine before saying evenly, 'We're talking about you Kit, not me. I don't pretend to have done everything right in my relationship with Noah. You more than anyone know how many stupid blunders I've made, but all that's in the past. I would follow him to the ends of the earth now if that's what it takes to keep him. I love him with every part of me.

'Is that how you love Jason? Will you go with him?'

I stare at Tory's serious face, not knowing the answer. Do I love Jason? The thought of losing him makes me feel sick. But am I prepared to walk away from my only family and my best friends to be with him?

'I don't know,' I whisper finally. 'I think I love him, but I don't know if I'm prepared to leave everything I've ever known to set up house with a man I've only been with for six months.'

'Tory stares at me for another couple of seconds, then something in my face makes her relent. 'You don't have to look as though the world's falling apart Kitty Kat. Maybe I'm being too hard on you. I just don't want you to make the same stupid mistakes I made, and risk losing everything because you're too entrenched in your beliefs to change. And anyway, you don't have to decide overnight do you? I'm sure Jason isn't holding a gun to your head quite yet.'

'Not yet,' I agree ruefully, 'But I can't string him along forever, and tomorrow night's the last time I'll see him for ten weeks. He's taken two months gardening leave to go back up and take care of Hugo.'

Tory frowns. 'Can't you go up with him? It would be a perfect opportunity to find if you could both make it work.' I'm shaking my head before she's finished. 'I have too many commitments here Tory. I might be able to get up for a weekend or something, but that's about it.'

'Did Jason say what he intends to do when he leaves the Navy?'

'I have no idea, we didn't get that far in the conversation. I think he's probably intending to drop another bombshell on me when we have dinner this evening. Maybe he'll turn the family pile into a theme park – with a name like Bloodstone Tower, he's bound to attract a lot of bloodthirsty tourists.' I sigh before continuing, 'Goodness knows what's going on in his head Tory. Whatever he decides to do, his house will take a packet to renovate and I don't think he's got that kind of money.'

At that moment our conversation is interrupted by a tiny mewling sound and I watch Tory's eyes immediately soften as she quickly gets up to check on her first born. Dotty is unceremoniously dumped onto the floor, and ever the opportunist, she immediately jumps into my lap.

'How's he sleeping?' I ask, glad to change the subject.

Tory grimaces as she picks up the tiny bundle. 'Not brilliant, but then it's so difficult to know if he's getting enough. This whole breast feeding lark is a bit of a lottery really. I seem to spend most of my time with one of my boobs hanging out.'

'A bit like me last night,' I quip before realizing I hadn't actually mentioned that part of the story. I busy myself stroking Dotty, hoping she was too taken up with Isaac to hear my comment. No such luck. After settling the little boy to her satisfaction, she looks up, eyes sparkling and simply says, 'Spill.'

Of course it was too much to hope for that my so called best friend would keep that little gem secret. She was still laughing when she left, and by six o'clock I was receiving topless pole dancing pictures from Freddy…

It's now seven and I'm about to leave the flat to meet Jason – of course this time my outfit bears more resemblance to a nun. I'm actually quite nervous about seeing him again. Not long after he delivered his bolt from the blue, he sent me home in a car. I would generally have stayed over, but, well with an Admiral in the house – especially one who'd already had an eyeful of my assets, it didn't really seem appropriate...

The evening is warm and sultry, making my navy blue polo neck dress stand out like a sore thumb compared to everyone else's summery pastels. As I make my way to The Royal Castle Hotel, I'm already uncomfortably warm. A quick glance at myself as I head into the dim interior and I groan inwardly. I look like I'm going to a bloody funeral. I sigh as I push open the door to the bar.

I never used to have this much trouble choosing clothes. Generally Kit Davies has always been a byword in Dartmouth for stylish and chic, but since losing the gallery last year, I seem to have lost my mojo a bit. Maybe I should consider burying myself in the wilds of Scotland before I turn into a bag lady.

I pause to look around the bar and quickly spot Jason near the window. He looks up as I approach and gives me a warm smile that turns my insides liquid. Sometimes I forget just how drop dead gorgeous he is. I lean down to give him a quick kiss, and as I straighten up, he eyes my dress up and down with a wry grin. 'Very, er, covered up,' he murmurs as I slide into the seat opposite.

Grimacing, I pull at the polo neck, trying to get some air to the area that saw far too much of it last night. 'See, I can dress conservatively when the occasion calls for it,' I say defensively.

'You look gorgeous as always, just, er, perfect for a casual evening at the pub,' is his deadpan response. I glare at him for a second before slumping back into my chair and pointing to the bottle already on ice. 'Pour me a drink before I expire from heat exhaustion.' With a grin he leans forward and manoeuvres the two empty glasses which I note are flutes. I assume he's bought Prosecco, but when he lifts the bottle from the bucket, I realize it's a little more than a simple sparkling wine.

'Champagne,' I murmur a little apprehensively, 'And a good one. Are we celebrating something?'

He fills the two glasses without speaking, then pushing one towards me, he raises his own glass. 'I'd really like to celebrate the start of a new exciting adventure for both of us.'

Feeling my heart do a double flip, I open my mouth to say something, despite the fact I have no idea what, but before I can speak, he leans forward and murmurs quietly, 'I know my words came as a bit of a shock last night, and perhaps I should have trodden a little more carefully, but Kit, I can't remember the last time I was so excited about a project.'

'You have a project?' I interject a little uneasily. 'I assume you're talking about renovating Bloodstone Tower?'

'Not just renovating,' is his animated response. 'I want to turn it into a boutique hotel, the kind of Bed and Breakfast that provides understated luxury for discerning guests in a friendly intimate atmosphere.'

'You sound as though you're reading from a brochure,' I quip feeling a slight frisson of excitement as his enthusiasm communicates itself to me, despite my misgivings. 'How will you do it?' I mean, it's er, not as though you're, er, awash with money – are you?' Maybe he's won the lottery and simply hasn't told me.

Jason takes a deep breath, and I sense that here is the clinker. 'I spoke to Noah a couple of weeks ago. I wanted to know if he'd be interested in investing – kind of like a sleeping partner.'

He spoke to Noah a couple of weeks ago. Why the hell didn't he tell me?

But in my heart I know why. The look on his face tells me exactly why he neglected to mention anything about it until now. Until he was prompted by his father's stroke. He thinks I'll turn him down. He's expecting to go up to Scotland alone.

I look down at my hands gripping my glass of Champagne, so tightly I'm in danger of cracking the glass. My mind is racing. I don't believe Tory knows anything about it – she wouldn't have kept something so monumental to herself.

'Is Noah interested?' My voice when I finally manage to speak sounds hollow and tinny. I look up and try to inject some enthusiasm in my voice. 'I mean, I assume he is, or we wouldn't be having this conversation.'

'He was very keen, so much so, he's agreed to finance the initial stage before the end of the year.'

'So what will he get out of it? Surely he's not doing it out of charity?' I don't even try to keep the sarcasm out of my voice and hate myself for it. Noah doesn't deserve my mockery, and the frown on Jason's face agrees.

'We'll be equal partners,' he answers eventually, 'But Noah has made it clear that he doesn't want any day to day involvement. We'll have a contract drawn up of course.'

I nod my head before taking a large gulp of Champagne and saying with false brightness, 'Well, it seems as though you've got everything sorted.'

'No not everything.' Jason's face is unsmiling as he takes my free hand gently. 'You're the most important piece Kit. I love you and want you to come with me.'

I don't know what to say. My heart is hammering like a construction worker. I take another gulp of Champagne, feeling the bubbles fizz up my nose. I can feel the panic begin to swamp me. Jason is waiting for an answer. Finally I look up.

'I don't know Jason. I..I'm sorry, but I can't give you any promises. I need more time to think about it.'

His face briefly tightens with disappointment, but then he controls his features, and with a smile, he squeezes my hand. 'Take all the time you need Kit. It would be good if you could come up for a weekend while I'm up there and I can show you exactly what's in my head?' He phrases his words as a question and I nod my head, no longer trusting myself to speak. If I say anything, I know I'll burst into tears.

Jason searches my face silently. No doubt my inner turmoil is pretty obvious and in the end, he gives my fingers one last squeeze before letting go. 'Shall we order?' he says, handing me the menu. His tone has reverted to business like and I'm torn between relief and anxiety that he's let the subject go so easily.

I stare blindly down at the menu. I need to get a grip. I don't know what's wrong with me. It's not as though he's asking me to go to bloody Outer Mongolia. It's Scotland for pity's sake - it's not even another country. Why am I so scared?

Chapter Four

I t's seven o'clock on Saturday morning and I really don't have any more time to dwell on big important life changing issues; I have one hundred penis shaped favours to turn into his and hers balloons, and three hours to do it in.

I've enlisted the help of Freddy, who's assured me he's a bit of an expert in penis shaped novelties. Obviously I've got to make sure that he knows I don't want them to look remotely phallic by the time we've finished. Tory wanted to come over and help too, but I gently told her to focus her energy on being a wonderful mum (it worked, although the truth is that Tory's about as artistic as a log with anything that doesn't involve curtains).

Dragging myself out of bed, I throw on some clothes and head into the lounge and the large box of chocolate todgers.

You may well ask why I didn't just order some more favours. Well bless them, the young couple are on a budget (that's why they hired me). Unfortunately the online company who made the error refused to send a hundred chocolate lolly pops until we'd returned the penises. With less than three days to go, that was obviously impossible, so I assured the hysterical bride to be that I would disguise our willies with some more melted chocolate, coloured marzipan and nuts (pardon the pun...) Easy peasy - I hope.

I'm determined not to get stressed out. The wedding's not until four o'clock this afternoon and everything else is pretty much good to go. It will just take a last minute walk round by yours truly to check that the hotel hasn't missed anything. I'll take the penises, sorry, balloons with me when I go.

Anyway, first things first, coffee – hot, strong, and lots of it.

Of course chopping up a hundred willies is probably not on most people's top ten ideas of how to spend their Saturday, but I'm actually quite glad to have something else to focus on besides my domestic issues.

Jason left my flat at five o'clock this morning after a truly amazing night of, well, passion. I know it sounds clichéd, but believe me he seemed determined to cram ten weeks of love making into one incredible night. We didn't talk at all, instead he showed me with his hands and his lips just how good we are together. Even now I can feel a warm tingle in the pit of my belly when I think about the way he moved over me, touching, stroking, caressing, until I could think of nothing else but the feel of him inside me.

'Sweetie, you've got that just laid look about you again. Please tell me it's not the thought of handling a mountain of chocolate peckers?'

I really shouldn't have given Freddy a key to my flat.

I resist the urge to rise to the bait and simply cast him a withering glance. 'Well that's the first, and hopefully the last penis joke of the morning. Do you want a coffee before we start?'

In the end it takes us nearly four hours, and by the time we finish, Freddy declares he's chopped up enough penises to potentially turn him into a murderous serial killer and will possibly need therapy. We have very cleverly (I think) used the testicles as the 'his and hers' balloons - one is covered in pink hundreds and thousands, the other in chopped nuts, (again, apologies...)

After covering the testicles (sorry balloons), we cut off the shaft which really made Freddy wince. I actually had a lot of fun eating the first few, but believe me you can get very sick of chocolate wedding tackle in a very short space of time.

Once we'd finished cutting and covering, we stuck a popsicle stick right up the middle of the balls (sorry balloons) and tied it off with gold ribbon (the bride's colour of choice). I mean come on, is that thinking outside the box or what?

We've laid them all on two massive trays I bought for the occasion, and if I say so myself, they don't look too bad at all, providing no one looks at them too closely – I'm hoping there'll be no guests who are experts on chocolate genitalia...

'Job well done Freddy,' I say, patting my rather pale assistant chocolatier on the back. Freddy makes a face. 'I don't think I'll be looking for a career as a mortician any time soon,' he murmurs with a small shudder.

'Come on I'll treat you to a bacon sandwich at Alf's before we load them into the car.'

'What part of a pig is bacon cut from?' he asks as we head down the stairs. 'The belly I think,' I answer laughing, 'Don't worry Freddy, you're not going to be eating any dangly bits.' As I open the door into the street, a sudden thought occurs to me. 'Did you know that a pig's orgasm lasts for thirty minutes? I read it on Facebook.'

Freddy stares at me for a second. 'I think I'll just have some cinnamon toast.'

Everything is set up. The hotel have done a grand job with the tables, and all that's left to do is grab the balloons from the car and place one on each napkin. As I head back out to my open boot, I notice a children's party in full swing in the adjacent room. Smiling, I stop at the open door to watch them at play. The hotel informed me of the party, assuring me that it will be finished well before the wedding party congregate for welcome drinks.

'Bloody hell, these balloons look like cocks, don't you fink Sharon?' My heart begins to thump as I hone in on a group of women sitting near the window.

'Dunno about that,' says a large woman who's obviously Sharon, 'Don't look nuffin like my Darren's meat and two veg, although come to think of it them balloons do look a bit like his balls after he'd had the snip. His left one swelled up just like that pink one.'

A cold feeling deep in my gut, I ignore the raucous laughter at the unfortunate Darren's expense and run quickly out to my car, just in time to see two little brats helping themselves to the last few of the favours I'd laboured so hard over. 'Why the hell didn't I shut the damn boot?' I mutter, resisting the urge to launch myself in a flying tackle at the little monster who's busy stuffing as many balloons as she can into her pocket.

'Oi,' I yell at the top of my voice instead, causing the little reprobate to drop the one she was just about to bite into. 'What on earth do you think you're doing?' I shout. The little girl takes one look at my furious face, and promptly bursts into tears.

'Ear, wot you doin' to my little girl?' Of course, she would be Sharon's offspring. Taking a deep breath, I turn round. 'Your child has just stolen these chocolate favours from the boot of my car.' My voice is positively bursting with righteous indignation.

'Well wot you leave the bloody boot open for?' she responds before turning towards her daughter who is now eying both of us calculatingly in between keeping up the noisy sobs. 'Chardonnay, did you nick this lady's chocolate balloons?' *Chardonnay??*

The brat's answer is to increase her wailing. If she doesn't end up in prison, this kid's got all the makings of an Oscar winning actress.

'Give 'em 'ere, now,' thunders her mother who doesn't look to have been taken in by her daughter's performance even remotely - which is more than I can say for all the interested spectators starting to gather.

Sharon holds out her hand, and after a very noticeable, though admittedly brief, internal battle, *Chardonnay* obviously decides that on this occasion she should quit while she's ahead. Taking a large defiant chunk out of the chocolate balloon she's holding, the future convict shuffles towards her mother, pulling the rest of the half melted favours out of her pocket.

Unfortunately, without their added toppings, they look even more like testicles, and as she hands over the gooey mess, Sharon gives a derogatory snort. 'If you ask me, my daughter's done you a good turn. They look more like balls than balloons, and I can't think of any bride who'd want a load of bollocks decorating her wedding tables.'

Chuckling at her own wit, she heads back inside with *Chardonnay* in tow, leaving me staring after them, now liberally covered in chocolate coated hundreds and thousands. To add insult to injury, the female Damian actually has the gall to turn round and stick her tongue out before disappearing through the door.

'Think you'll need to get that dress cleaned,' offers one helpful onlooker and I gamely resist the childish urge to throw the chocolate balls at her, just so I can say, 'Now yours does too.'

I glance down at my watch. Three o'clock – one hour to go, and I admit I'm fresh out of ideas. I briefly debate whether to see if I can salvage any of the other favours that have obviously already made it into the children's party, but I finally accept defeat. Dartmouth's about ten minutes drive away so at least I have time to go home and change.

Wearily, I belatedly close the boot to my car, but just as I start walking round to the driver's side, a young woman comes running towards me, a large box held awkwardly in front of her.

'I heard what happened,' she pants breathlessly when she finally reaches my side. 'I thought you might want these.' She opens the top of the box so I can peer inside. Nestling in layers of tissue paper are exquisitely wrapped mini boxes of chocolates. 'There are a hundred and fifty. Will that be enough?' I look up at my saviour, completely lost for words. 'They were left over from our conference yesterday,' she continues with a smile, 'I was just going to take them home and dish them out to my family, but I think your need is definitely greater than mine.' This time I don't resist the childish urge to hug her.

The little boxes looked delightful on the tables, and if they had *Taylor Roofing* stamped on the bottom, well by the time any of the guests noticed, they were too well oiled to care…

~*~

Admiral Charles Shackleford was a troubled man. It wasn't

often his conscience bothered him, although he had to say there appeared to have been a worrying increase in dialogue between his brain and his scruples in recent months. Right now, he was feeling something worse: Guilt.

Hugo Buchannan was one of his oldest friends – in actual fact, while he was on the subject of soul searching, he had to admit the irascible Scot was probably one of his only friends. The other one was Jimmy. It was therefore quite fitting when he thought about it, that he was waiting for one to talk about the other.

He was sitting on his usual bar stool at The Ship, his watering hole of choice – although that might also have to do with the fact that he'd been banned from most of the other pubs within a three mile radius. Pickles was snoozing happily at his feet and the Admiral would have been perfectly content with the world had it not been for this blasted conscience which had been showing far too bloody much of itself lately.

There was no doubt, he was going soft. He wasn't sure if it was Mabel's influence or the arrival of the new rug rat. Either way, he hadn't had a decent night's sleep since he'd heard about Hugo's stroke, wondering whether the bloody shenanigans last year had had something to do with his friend's unfortunate decline in health.

At that moment – just in the nick of time the Admiral privately thought as he wasn't a man given to excessive introspection – Jimmy Noon pushed open the pub door, bringing with him the damp earthy smell of the English Summer. The Admiral nodded to his friend and pointed to the pint already waiting on the bar.

'How's Tory and the baby?' Jimmy asked a trifle breathlessly as he levered himself up onto his stool. 'Emily went over to visit the other day and she told me what a gorgeous little boy he is. She said Victory looked radiant.'

The Admiral frowned. 'Why did you ask the damned question if you already knew the bollocking answer?' he demanded irritably.

'You must be very proud Sir,' Jimmy continued, ignoring his former commanding officer's grouchy response. Experience told him that he wouldn't have to wait long to find out what was souring the Admiral's mood this time, and he resolved to simply enjoy his pint in the meantime.

At length the Admiral sighed, causing Jimmy to feel the familiar fluttering of anxiety in the pit of his stomach.

'You've heard about old Scotty?' he said and the small man nodded his head. 'You were the one who told me Sir. How is he?'

'Well he hasn't popped his clogs yet,' the Admiral responded, irritable at the implication that he might have forgotten their last conversation – which he had. Unfortunately he had to admit, if only privately, that his memory had been playing him up a bit lately.

'Thing is Jimmy lad...' Here it comes thought Jimmy as the Admiral paused to take a long draft of his beer. 'The thing is....' Another halt, causing Jimmy's alarm bells to start clanging insistently.

Totally oblivious to his friend's consternation, the Admiral finally finished in a rush, 'The thing is, I can't help but wonder if the bit of a problem we had last year might have had something to do with... you know... with old Hugo's date with the scab lifter.'

Jimmy stared at his friend in astonishment. The Admiral had what could only be described as a look of fear on his face. This was such an unprecedented turn of events that Jimmy was, for a few moments, rendered completely speechless. The Admiral shook his head sadly, mistaking Jimmy's silence for acquiescence. 'I know Jimmy lad, you're right, I couldn't have put it more plainly myself.

'Well, it can't helped, Mabel and Emily are going to just have to accept it.'

'Accept what?' asked Jimmy, still reeling from the thought that the Admiral was actually worried about someone else. Very worried indeed.

'Come on Jimmy keep up,' Charles Shackleford responded impatiently, waving at the barman to bring them both a refill. 'It's obvious. We're the ones who nearly got Scotty juggling halos, so it stands to reason it's our job to nurse him back from the brink...'

Chapter Five

It's Monday evening and I'm knackered. To be fair, it's a good knackered. Saturday's wedding went off smoothly without any more references to wedding tackle, chocolate or otherwise. Mr. Smeelie's funeral was a suitably respectful if sombre affair after I managed to bribe the printers to correct the small, though crucial spelling mistake on the order of service. I've now promised them first dibs at doing the service booklets for little Isaac's christening, which I assured them will definitely be happening in the not too distant future.

I have no doubt it will take place sometime before he's twenty one.

So now, with all work related issues dealt with, I'm back to waiting for Jason to call and stressing over whether I'm really up for an eight hundred mile move to a heap of ruins in the wilds of Scotland. I really want to call Tory, but there's a new unwritten rule – no phone calls between four pm and eight pm due to Isaac's bath time routine. I glance down at my watch. Six thirty, so another one and a half hours until I can bend her ear. Although to honest she tends to resemble an extra off *The Walking Dead* once her first born's in bed, so I'm unlikely to get much in the way of solid advice.

The fact is, I've not actually gotten around to telling her about Jason's plans to renovate Bloodstone Tower yet, and I've not quite worked up the nerve to speak to Noah about his potential involvement. It all feels so unreal, and perhaps if I don't say anything, I can convince myself it's not happening.

Of course there's one other person I could talk to. Aunt Flo has always come up trumps when it comes to giving wise counsel. Maybe I should phone her. Another crisis might just be the ticket to biting off the first tiny chunks of the elephant in the room.

Taking a deep breath, I call her number. I have no idea why my heart is beating so fast or hard, it's not like we haven't spoken over the last few months. The problem is, it's never been about anything remotely important. We've been like two acquaintances who bump into each other every Sunday at church. I half hope she's not in, but after a few more seconds, just when I'm about to put down the phone, my aunt answers.

'Aunt Flo, it's me, Kit.' My voice sounds a bit faint, almost breathless. There's an imperceptible pause on the other end before Aunt Flo answers, her voice as warm and welcoming as always. 'Sweetheart, lovely to hear from you. How's your business going?'

I feel the tears gather in my eyes at the kindness in her tone, and have to fight the urge to break down and bawl down the phone like a child. Instead I swallow convulsively and focus on her question. 'All going quite well actually except for a couple of hiccups this weekend.' Then I find myself telling her the story about the chocolate penises and poor old Mr Smeelie's order of service. Before long Flo is laughing ribaldry down the phone and it feels almost like old times. Almost.

'So what about you and Jason?' she goes on to say eventually, catching me off guard. 'How's your relationship with the dashing captain going?' I take a deep breath before saying impulsively. 'Are you busy? Can I come over and see you this evening?'

'Of course sweetheart, you're always welcome, you know that. Why don't you stay over and I'll open a bottle of wine? Have you eaten yet? I have a big pot of chilli simmering on the stove and there's far too much for me and Pepé.'

Ten minutes later I'm driving through Stoke Fleming feeling as though a lead weight has been lifted off my shoulders. I determine there and then that I will no longer allow the issue of my barking mad father to get between me and the one person who's loved me since the day I was born. If Aunt Flo left me with her brother and his wife, she must have had a damn good reason. She would never have done it otherwise. Maybe she'll tell me, maybe she won't, but I'm so tired of the rift between us.

As I pull into Flo's drive, my aunt comes to the door, Pepé in her arms. As soon as he sees me get out of the car, the little dog immediately squirms to get down, running up to me barking joyfully and giving my leg a happy little hump.

'Hi Peps,' I murmur, bending down to pry him off my leg and give him a fuss. Mating with any available appendage is Pepé's way of saying hello. It's mostly endearing, but occasionally bloody embarrassing...

I walk towards my aunt who's remained by the door. Her stance is slightly wary, but there's a warm smile on her face. As I reach her, she searches my face then holds out her arms. With a small sob, I allow myself to be folded in her familiar embrace.

After a few seconds, she pushes me away from her to look back at my face. 'Something's wrong sweetheart,' she states matter of factly. 'Come in and tell me about it.' Then, putting her arm around my shoulders, she guides me into the cosy interior of her cottage.

It's well past nine before we finish supper, and as usual, Flo insisted that conversation while we ate be kept light and fluffy to aid digestion. In her opinion, important matters are best discussed over coffee and liqueurs. Her cooking was as eclectic as always and I could swear there were prawns in my chilli con carne. We ate sitting outside on the patio, overlooking the breathtaking beauty of Blackpool Sands, and basking in the warmth of the late evening sun.

Now as the sun begins to dip below the horizon, it's turning a little chilly, and Flo comes back with blankets to go with our Irish coffees. Wrapping mine gratefully around me, I reflect ruefully that she obviously thinks we're going to be here for some time. Taking a sip of my coffee, I look down to see Pepé whining softly at my side, and lifting up one side of the blanket, I pat my knee. Without hesitation, he jumps up and settles himself under the cover with a small contented sigh. If only life was that simple...

'So sweetheart, what's bothering you?' Predictably my aunt comes straight to the point and I look down at my cup before answering.

'Jason's leaving the RN,' I say eventually, still staring down into my coffee dregs.

'Is that such a bad thing?' she asks softly, and the slight confusion colouring her question causes me to look up and shake my head.

'It's not that. God knows I'm not really cut out to be the partner of a naval officer.' I cringe as I remember the First Sea Lord's dinner. 'It's what he wants to do instead.'

Flo waits without speaking and with a sigh I tell her about Jason's plans to revamp his family home.

'The thing is, he wants me to go with him,' I finish in a rush. 'I mean, he won't actually move for another few months, but he wants to get the ball rolling as soon as possible. Noah's not exactly short of cash and I think he's given Jason carte blanch to do whatever he thinks necessary.'

'Wow,' Aunt Flo murmurs softly when it's clear I've nothing else to add. 'It's an amazing opportunity sweetheart, and very exciting.' She pauses and leans forward to peer at me in the gathering dusk before continuing drily, 'Although I have to say you have the same look on your face now as you did when you found out you had to have your appendix out.'

I bend forward and wrap my arms around Pepé's softly snoring outline. 'You know me Aunt Flo, I hate change, and this one's a whopper. What if I up sticks, move all that way and it doesn't work out between me and Jason? What if I hate Scotland? The weather's awful and there are those horrible black midgey things that get everywhere. What if he wants me to do the cooking? You know I hate cooking – the only one worse than me at it is Tory. What if I...?' I finally grind to a halt as I catch my aunt shaking her head ruefully. 'How can I leave all my friends Aunt Flo?' I finish softly, the tears finally flowing, 'How can I leave you?'

'Sweetheart, you're not thinking of going to the other side of the world. It's Scotland, not the Gobi Desert; and you're not leaving your friends. Do you think Tory would ever let you leave her for good? I mean her husband is going to be involved for goodness sake. And Freddy? Come on Kit, you know Freddy, he'd be in if he fell in...

'And as for me, well, you couldn't pay enough to keep me away. I haven't had so much excitement since I sold my first book, and I wouldn't mind having a hotty in a kilt as my next fictional hero. The Scottish Highlands will be just the place to get my creative juices flowing.'

Her words simply serve to make me cry harder, and at my distraught wailing, Pepé pops his head anxiously out of the nest he's made. Cuddling him to me I rock backwards and forwards, allowing the tears to track unheeded down my face. I don't even know any longer what I'm crying for. It's as though everything that's happened since I lost the gallery has culminated at this precise point.

As I sob into Pepé's increasingly soggy fur, Aunt Flo just hands me a tissue and sits quietly, giving me time and space to get myself together.

Finally, just before Pepé needs to start paddling, my sobs turn into hiccupping gulps, and my gulps into sighs. Lifting my head up, I blow my nose into the sodden tissue. 'I'm so sorry,' I murmur jerkily, 'I have no idea where all that came from.'

Without answering, Aunt Flo gets up and busies herself turning on the heater and lighting candles to banish the gloom. By the time I've finished mopping myself up, we're surrounded by soft flickering candlelight, and the warmth of the electric heater is doing wonders towards drying Pepé's fur. Aunt Flo disappears into the house just as the last of the sun's rays vanishes over the horizon, leaving the sea to merge in with the sky, now a mysterious dark purple.

Sighing, I snuggle down into my wrap, enjoying the brief feeling of weightlessness that comes after a good cry. After a couple of minutes, my aunt returns with another bottle of wine and two glasses.

'It's time for us to have that talk sweetheart.'

~*~

Jason Buchannan finally turned off the engine and sagged wearily back into his seat. He didn't know what the actual time was but he knew it was late. The almost perpetual twilight that passed for night this far north during the summer months made it a little disorientating. Glancing down at his watch, he groaned. Eleven thirty. Probably too late to call Kit now.

He'd been at the hospital for most of the day and it was becoming increasingly obvious that he wouldn't be able to bring his father home without someone to look after him full time – at least for the first couple of months. The problem was, getting someone to come to such a remote location was going to be tough in itself – without the added complications of Bloodstone Tower's less than salubrious facilities. Jason ruefully eyed the pile of bricks in front of him. The alternative was to put his father in a nursing home, and he just couldn't do it. Jason had never seen his father look so vulnerable and actually found himself wondering if Hugo Buchannan had always been that small.

Sighing, he finally got out of the car and headed round the back to the kitchen entrance. The light was still on in the archaic cavern which housed their cooking facilities, and through the window Jason could see Aileen sitting at the table. Frowning he noted there was someone with her. That was all he needed – more small talk. Grimacing, he let himself in and tried to plaster a smile on his face as the two seated women turned to face him.

'Weir ya been laddy? I was proper riled – thought you might've ended up in the loch somewhere.' Aileen got to her feet as she spoke and headed over to the kettle. 'There's a wee dram on the table to go wi ya coffee,' she threw over her shoulder as she poured in some more water from the sink.

'You're a star Aileen,' Jason murmured, relaxing for the first time that day. Sitting down at the table he poured himself a large whiskey and took an appreciative sip. The occupant of the other chair eyed him curiously, but both waited patiently for Aileen to make the introductions.

'This here's ma niece Nicole, she's up fro' London for a short holiday.'

Jason smiled wearily, 'Hi Nicole from London, is this your first visit to The Highlands?'

Nicole gave an answering smile. 'No, I've been here lots of time, but not for a while. I think the last time was when I was twelve wasn't it Aileen?'

'Aye, about that,' responded her aunt, returning to the table to place Jason's coffee in front of him.

Jason eyed the girl sitting opposite curiously. She didn't look much older than twelve now truth be told and he certainly couldn't remember having seen her here before. He would never have forgotten hair as red as hers or eyes as big and green. With her petite build, she reminded him of a small sprite and looked as though she belonged more in the woods than here in a kitchen.

'Are you staying here?' he asked as the silence began to stretch, 'I mean it's not a problem,' he added hastily, not wanting to insinuate that she wasn't welcome. God knows if she was prepared to put up with the archaic plumbing and his wandering grandmother, she was welcome to stay. Another pair of hands never hurt.

Aileen shoved a plate of homemade shortbread in front of him. 'Nicole just wanted to get out of the city for a while, get a bit of peace and quiet, and I tol' her to come straight up here. You don't get more quiet and peaceful than Bloodstone Tower.' Jason grimaced. 'And therein lies the problem,' he muttered ruefully.

'You want to talk about it laddy?' Aileen asked matter of factly, 'How's the laird doing?'

Hugo Buchannan was not really Lord of anything, but Aileen

had been here as long as Jason could remember, and throughout that time she persisted in calling his father by a title that no longer existed.

'He's improving slowly,' Jason grunted, taking another sip of his whisky, 'But it's going to be a while before he's back on his feet, and until then he's going to need someone to look after him. Not an easy task I'm afraid,' he continued waving at the kitchen around him.

He hadn't yet confided his plans for the Tower to his father or Aileen, and he wasn't sure how either would take it. His father would be delighted to have him back home full time, but the old man lived in cloud cuckoo land when it came to finances. And then there was Kit. He had no idea whether she would get behind his plans for their future, and he wasn't sure if he was prepared to go ahead without her by his side.

'I could help you out for a while.' The small voice from his side brought him out of his reverie and he looked down at Nicole with the first burgeoning of hope.

'I can't stay for longer than a couple of months,' the petite woman continued, 'But I have some first aid training and would be happy to help your father get back on his feet while you look for someone more permanent. I'm sure Aileen and I could cope between us.'

Jason looked over at the two women. Aileen was nodding her agreement, and for the first time that day he felt the band of almost panic constricting his chest begin to ease.

'That would be amazing if you could, at least in the short term,' Jason responded, not bothering to hide the relief in his voice, 'I'll pay you of course.'

Nicole smiled in answer. 'You don't need to pay me, just put me up and feed me and I'll be perfectly content. I love the tranquility of Bloodstone Tower, it's exactly what I need right now.' Jason smiled back, wondering what had driven her to leave London. 'Well you'll get that in spades,' he murmured finishing his whisky, 'We'll talk more in the morning if you don't mind, right now I'm absolutely exhaus...'

A sudden commotion outside caused him to pause, frowning. Spike the cat was yowling, hissing and spitting outside the kitchen window at what appeared to be a stray dog if the noise of barking and growling was anything to go by.

'What the blo...?' Jason broke off as the kitchen door was thrown open, allowing Spike to dash in, closely followed by a large Springer spaniel. Jason's heart dropped into his feet.

'You're going to have to do something about that bloody bag of fur and bones or Pickles is likely to have him for his bollocking breakfast one of these days.'

Jason stared in horrified disbelief as the large figure of Charles Shackleford appeared in the open doorway.

'Don't worry lad, your problems are over,' the Admiral boomed, casting a benevolent glance towards the three startled faces staring at him from the table. 'I'm here to do my bit to keep old Scotty on this mortal coil for a tad longer, and Jimmy'll be up here tomorrow to do his bit. One look at us and your dad'll be on his feet in no time, just you wait and see...'

Chapter Six

Aunt Flo pours the wine and hands me the first glass without speaking. Then, seating herself back in the chair opposite, she puts a blanket over her knees and stares down at her drink for a few seconds. When she finally looks up, her expression is set and determined.

'I think we've both put off having this conversation for far too long Kit, but things need to be said and I'm afraid we're beginning to run out of time to say them.' She pauses and I frown, alarmed at the sense of finality in her voice, but before I can open my mouth, she holds up her hand. 'Please sweetheart, let me speak. I've rehearsed these words in my head so many times, and if I'm ever to have a good night's sleep again, I need to get them off my chest.

'As you know, I escaped from your father's control with the help of Charles Shackleford's friend Boris... er... good God, I don't even know his second name.' She sighs irritably before continuing, 'Unfortunately your father, Luke, was injured in the process.'

'Don't you mean killed?' I interrupt, unable to help myself. Aunt Flo frowns before dropping her bombshell. 'What makes you think your father was killed?'

I stare at her without speaking, completely blindsided by her revelation.

'Kit your father isn't dead; he's still very much alive. That's why I had to stay away from you for so long.'

~*~

Tory ran her hands through her hair and glanced at the clock. Three thirty in the morning. Throwing the covers back, she climbed out of bed, weariness making her stumble as she made her way to Isaac's crib situated a few feet away. 'Hey little man,' she whispered to her son who gave no sign of having heard his mother, being too intent on screaming the house down.

'Come on sweetie pie, let's get you fed.' Leaning down, she scooped up the red-faced bundle and turned back towards the bed where her eyes lit on the side that was Noah's, empty but for a disgruntled Dotty.

Her husband was in London for the premier of *Nocturne*. The Science Fiction movie Noah had been working on during their brief break up over last summer was finally having its premier in London's Leicester Square. Tory had hoped she'd be able to attend the glittering event alongside Noah, but the small bundle in her arms dictated otherwise.

Sighing she began feeding Isaac, her mind going back to the TV coverage of the premier that had been shown earlier. Noah had looked absolutely stunning as he always did in a dinner jacket, and she'd felt the familiar stab of anxiety coupled with a sense of unreality that always swamped her whenever they weren't together. There were the usual bevy of beautiful women surrounding him, and after ten minutes, she'd switched the program off and taken herself off to bed.

Looking down at her son now, she bent her head and whispered, 'Don't worry little man, daddy loves us best.' Tory hoped it was true.

~*~

'But, I thought you shot him?' My voice is husky with shock.

My aunt nods her head. 'I did, and believe me, at the time I thought I'd killed him. In fact, I hoped I had.' Her voice in contrast to mine is scathing and angry. 'But I should have known better. The bastard recovered after a few months in hospital.

'You and I were living in a flat in Bristol during that period and I lived in total fear that he would decide to press charges and I'd be dragged back to the States to answer for what I'd done.

'But of course that wasn't your father's style. He was all about control, and he still wanted control of me and more importantly, you Kit. I knew he wouldn't rest until he'd tracked us both down, but the only way he could find you was through me.

'I changed your name and we stayed off the grid as far as possible. My father had died while I was in America, but my mother was still alive. When I finally ran out of money, I contacted her and she set up a standing order that kept us both off the streets. She didn't know the whole story, but she knew enough not to ask where I was living.'

Aunt Flo pauses, closing her eyes briefly, and when she continues, her voice is filled with bitter regret. 'I never saw my mother again, but I made the mistake of going to her funeral. I only stayed for one night and left you back in Bristol with a friend.'

'Who?' I butt in, wanting – needing – to know everything now the can of worms has finally been opened. My aunt shook her head. 'It doesn't matter. It's what happened while I was in Dartmouth that matters.' She stops again, grimacing as the memories come flooding back. 'While I was here, I bumped into Luke's parents and found out he was on his way back to the UK. It was obvious they didn't know exactly what had happened between the two of us, and more importantly they had no idea their son had fathered a child.

'They were however, very aware of the scandal their son had caused during his time in Charleston and that disgrace had somehow found its way back to the wealthy Dartmothians, to such an extent that Luke's parents found themselves ostracized by their peers and were busy relocating to Brighton to escape the shame.

'In a panic, I rushed back to Bristol. I had no idea what to do, but knew I had to protect you at all costs.' She takes a long gulp of her wine, but this time in the interim I say nothing, engrossed in the story. It feels like just that – a story. One that happened to someone else.

My aunt takes a deep breath and continues, 'My brother Gareth had left Dartmouth along with his childhood sweetheart when I was still a teenager – even all those years ago they both had itchy feet.' She pauses, grimacing slightly before continuing, 'My brother was the lucky one – he managed to escape our father much earlier than me.

'We weren't close, I heard nothing from him while I was in the States and neither of them came home for mum's funeral. However, one of Gareth's oldest friends did. He told me he'd heard that Gareth and Sylvia had got married and were living in the Midlands. He gave me my brother's contact details, and in desperation, I called him when I got back to Bristol.

'We met up in Gloucester and I told him everything that had happened. At the time he seemed like an answer to my prayers.' She looks over at me and her face is filled with sorrow. 'His wife had lost a child – a girl – a year earlier, and they'd been told by doctors there would be no more. Apparently, Sylvia had taken it harder than my brother.

'You were still young, not even three years old. It seemed like the perfect solution – even though it broke my heart to let you go.' I stare mutely at her face, vaguely registering that her features are a mask of anguish, and feel a lump come into my throat.

'The deal was that they passed you off as their own,' Aunt Flo whispers into the silence. 'After a few months in Nottingham, they returned to Dartmouth with no one the wiser. I went to London, and that's when I started writing.'

'But what about my moth… Sylvia's parents?' I ask, 'They were still alive then weren't they? Didn't they know that I wasn't their natural grandchild?'

'They didn't ask,' Aunt Flo responded wearily, 'I think they were so glad to have their daughter back, they didn't question the cock and bull story that Sylvia and Gareth fed them.' My aunt pauses and looks over at me with a slight smile. 'They loved you very much Kit. I think if they'd lived longer, things might have been very different.

'Sylvia was never very maternal. I don't think she ever looked on you as her own. Perhaps my brother did, in the beginning, but when his wife's parents died, his wander lust returned and you became an encumbrance that kept them in one place.'

'Is that why you came back?' I ask, unable to help myself.

My aunt sighs before speaking. 'Luke – your father – managed to track me down in London as I knew he would, but by then he was a shadow of his former self. His injury – the injury I'd inflicted on him – had taken its toll on his health and he was no longer the charismatic man he'd once been. He very nearly convinced me that he'd changed completely and I was so close to telling him where you were.' I feel my heart constrict painfully at the thought that I might have had an opportunity to know my real father, but at her next words, that brief daydream died without really being born.

'When I told him you'd been adopted,' he beat me with his walking stick, and I think he would have killed me if he hadn't been stopped by the man who'd recently become my agent.'

'Neil,' I breathe and she nods. 'He saved my life that day, and very possibly yours. Luke was arrested and spent the next three years in jail. While he was there, he had a stroke – possibly caused by being shot in the head by yours truly.' My aunt's voice shows no remorse or pity towards the man who'd caused her so much anguish. 'The last I heard he was living with his parents in Brighton.'

'Didn't he tell the police what had happened in the States when they arrested him?' I ask, not because I think he deserved any leniency, but the fact that he'd nearly beaten my aunt to death indicated that he wasn't exactly a man to let bygones be bygones.

'I think he was afraid it would go worse for him if he dragged up everything that happened in the US. At the end of the day, his sentence for committing grievous bodily harm was fairly lenient. He thought he'd be out in three years to continue his reign of terror. But it wasn't to be.' The only inflection in her voice as she finishes, is one of satisfaction, and I can't blame her for that.

'I came back when I knew he couldn't hurt you anymore,' Aunt Flo continues, her voice softening. 'I was horrified by the way Gareth and Sylvia had treated you and I did my best to make it up to you.' She pauses and holds out her hand. I take it, watching bemused at the tears running down her face. 'I'm so sorry,' she whispers, 'Everything I did, I did out of love for you, to keep you safe.

'I bought this cottage and did my damndest to make sure you spent as much time here as possible. I should have told you the truth, but it never seemed to be the right time. Can you ever forgive me?' Her voice breaks and she muffles a sob with her other hand.

Tipping Pepé unceremoniously from my lap, I jump up to enfold her in my arms. 'There's nothing to forgive,' I murmur gruffly, my own voice rough with unshed tears. 'There's only one person to blame in this whole sorry mess and that's the madman who sired me. But he's got exactly what he deserves and I'm so glad I can't remember him.'

I stroke her hair, holding her as she weeps. 'You've been my mother and father Aunt Flo, in every way that really counts, and I have no wish to ever see that bastard.' My voice is vehement and passionate, but there's a small voice in the back of my head that's asking if the last bit is genuinely true…

~*~

The sun was streaming in the windows when Tory woke up again. Dotty was spooning her and it was a wonder her snores hadn't woken up Isaac.

Oh my God, Isaac! Tory shot up in bed and ran over to the crib, only to breathe a sigh of relief at the sight of her son's big blue eyes gazing up at her seriously. Picking him up, she padded back to the bed, laying him gently on his changing mat so she could change his nappy before feeding him. Dotty sat up and stretched, giving a small sniff to the baby's head.

Contrary to everyone's concerns that she might feel her nose put out of joint, the little dog appeared to adore the Isaac and spent much of her time sitting as close to him as possible. Now however, it was clearly well before her preferred getting up time, and, after a token lick on his forehead, Dotty snuggled back down in the covers with a small sigh.

Smiling, Tory deftly changed the little boy's nappy and, leaning back against the headboard, prepared to feed him. Grabbing the remote, she switched on the TV before settling her son to his satisfaction. The news was on, but Tory, bending her head to add her own kiss to his delectable forehead, wasn't watching. Suddenly though, she heard Noah's name and she glanced up, thinking it was about last night's movie premier.

Instead there was a lurid photo of her husband and Gaynor Andrews, his former lover, locked in what appeared to be a passionate clinch. Distantly Tory could hear the reporter's voice over as she stared in shock at the graphic photograph.

'Is Noah Westbrook's fairytale marriage over? This photograph, splashed all over Social Media, was taken in the early hours of this morning after last night's premier of his new movie, and it most definitely suggests that the actor may well have fallen back into the arms of his former love interest, actress Gaynor Andrews...'

Chapter Seven

'**B**loody hell, is there nothing to eat in this bollocking mausoleum? No wonder old Scotty prefers it in hospital.'

Jason clenched his jaw as the Admiral's strident tones echoed into the great hall from the kitchen where he'd evidently been looking for some breakfast. Glancing down at his watch, Jason registered that it was seven thirty in the morning. He'd been up all night looking at his father's accounts. Throwing down his pen wearily, he stood up and stretched before reluctantly heading towards his uninvited guest.

'Aileen doesn't start until eight,' he said through gritted teeth as he entered the kitchen, 'If you can wait a while, I'm sure she'd be delighted to show you some good old Scottish hospitality.'

The Admiral glanced round with a loud humph, before stomping off towards the back door with Pickles in tow. Without bothering to say anything further, he threw open the door and slammed it behind him, leaving Jason staring open mouthed. Obviously not a morning person.

Shaking his head, Jason headed over to make a pot of coffee. After breakfast he intended to head over to the hospital to talk about his father's rehabilitation.

He wasn't sure whether to laugh or cry at the Admiral's offer to care for his old friend. If anything, the Admiral's nursing style was more likely to ensure that his father cashed in his chips at the first opportunity. Sighing, he put the problem of Charles Shackleford to the back of his mind to be dealt with later. He would call Mabel this afternoon to see if she could persuade her headstrong husband to come home. Failing that, he'd have to resort to Tory, or possibly commit murder...

Pouring himself a strong black coffee, he headed back to his desk in the Great Hall. He wasn't sure how his father would take the idea of turning his beloved pile of bricks into a luxury hotel, but Jason knew they'd have to have the conversation as soon as Hugo was strong enough. Financially, things were much worse than Jason had thought, and if they were to stand any chance of saving the family home, then it was imperative that the work began as soon as possible. They would need to be up and running before the start of the following summer and his termination date.

Seating himself back at his desk, Jason found his thoughts drifting to Aileen's niece Nicole. She'd seemed very pleasant, not to mention almost eager to help with his father. Frowning slightly, he remembered the small woman's quick offer of assistance, and her admission that she needed the tranquility of Bloodstone Tower. He couldn't help wondering if there was something she was running away from.

~*~

I wake up to the insistent ringing of my mobile phone. Jason. After trying briefly to sit up, I collapse back down against the pillows wincing at the throbbing in my head. Overindulgence of both wine and tears are two things definitely calculated to leave you with a thick head the next morning.

Groaning, I reach out and manage to snag the offending device, holding it in front of my face as I squint, trying to read the name of the caller. Not Jason, but Tory. I glance at the time – it's only six thirty for goodness sake. Then my heart stutters. If she's calling this early, there must be something wrong. Headache forgotten, I quickly sit up in bed and answer her call.

'Hey sweetie, is Isaac okay?'

'Turn on your TV,' she states without preamble, her voice edgy and anxious. Feeling an answering tug, I shake my head before realizing she can't see me. 'I'm at Aunt Flo's,' I say instead, 'She doesn't have a TV in the bedroom. Why, what's wrong?'

To my dismay, her response is a small sob and I grip the phone as fear suddenly swamps me.

'Is there something wrong with Isaac?' I all but shout when she doesn't speak. I can practically feel her gather herself together on the other end of the phone and a loud wail in the background alleviates my fear that something dreadful has happened to her son.

'No, Isaac's fine,' she finally murmurs, boosting my feeling of relief – until her next words.

'It's Noah. I think he's seeing Gaynor again...'

I manage to get to Tory's within half an hour, and in one piece too – always a bonus. I left a quick note for Aunt Flo and crept out without waking her, then drove like a bat out of hell along the narrow country lanes back to Dartmouth. Once on the ferry, I logged on to Facebook, scrolling down to see if I could find the pictures that Tory was referring to. Unfortunately, it was all too easy and I felt my heart hammer in anger as I examined the grainy photograph. It was definitely Noah and Gaynor, but if truth be told, it was difficult to see whether they were having a full blown episode including tongues, or simply kissing goodbye. Starting up my engine as we arrived at the other side, I really hoped it was the latter at that time in the morning.

So now, I park the car and, using the key they gave me, I push open the door to Tory and Noah's sumptuous house. Dotty greets me with a welcoming bark on the other side, but there's no sign of Tory and the baby. After a quick glance in the drawing room and kitchen, I head upstairs, finally tracking my best friend down in the nursery.

Curled up in a chair, she looks up as I enter, her face almost ashen. I run forward and crouch down, leaning forward to give her a hug.

'You know it's all a load of bollocks don't you Tory?' She nods her head against mine and I lean back to search her face.

'I felt so sick at first,' she admits, 'That's when I panicked and called you – I couldn't get hold of Noah.' She takes a deep breath before continuing, 'He wouldn't cheat on me Kit, and especially not with Gaynor. It's just... I hate all this. It's almost like people want him to do it. They actually want him to fall off the damn pedestal they put him on in the first place. How long will it be before the vultures start gathering again? I can't keep running every time the going gets a little rough.'

'They'll soon bugger off when they realize there's no story. You know what the paparazzi are like – if you're not crying into your vodka or wandering around in a daze looking like a vagrant, they'll start looking for something or someone more interesting to photograph.'

'Come on, it's too early to hit the hard stuff, so let's leave Isaac to his nap and go and grab some caffeine.'

Ten minutes later we're tucking into coffee and croissants. 'It's amazing how averting potential catastrophes makes you hungry,' Tory mumbles with her mouth full. I nod, bending down to give my last piece of to Dotty who is in imminent danger of doing an impromptu somersault in her efforts to get closer to the food source.

Suddenly Tory's mobile rings and glancing down, she almost chokes trying to swallow the last piece of her croissant. 'It's Noah,' she manages to wheeze before swiping her finger across the front of the phone and treating her beloved to a coughing fit worthy of someone who's smoked forty a day for most of their life. Finally, she hands the phone over to me, indicating I should talk.

'Hi Noah,' I say drily as my friend continues to sound like a parrot being strangled. 'Your other half is fine – it's just a croissant went down the wrong way.'

'As you're at the house at seven thirty in the morning, I take it you've seen the photo?' he responds, his voice matter of fact with an undertone of anger. 'Oh yes,' I reply, 'It's a lovely one of Gaynor. Can't really see your face, but you're both certainly looking very wrapped up in each other.'

'You know it's a fake Kit,' is his dry response, 'So cut the crap and put my wife on.' I laugh and hand over the phone. After a few more splutters, Tory is able to hold a conversation and I watch her mood visibly lighten as she speaks to her husband.

Leaving her to it, I wander into the drawing room, drawn to the huge bi-fold doors and the magnificent view beyond. The sun is casting early morning shadows over the sloping lawn and dancing on the surface of the river below, causing it to glint with tiny sparkles. The scene is almost too beautiful to be real and I feel a lump come into my throat. How can I leave this?

I feel as though I'm standing on the edge of a cliff where every path down to safety is fraught with potential pain and heartache. Squeezing my eyes shut against the halcyon vision in front of me, I wearily lean my head against the already warm glass.

I just want things to go back to the way they were before Jason decided to up sticks and move to the middle of nowhere, and before I learned that my father is still alive...

~*~

Jimmy couldn't believe he was actually sitting on a train on his way to Scotland. How the bloody hell had the Admiral managed to convince him that what happened to Hugo was in fact partly his fault? He shook his head in bemusement and wondered what Emily would have to say when she eventually found out he wasn't just going up for the weekend to see his old friend, but could actually be away for a couple of weeks – or even longer.

His heart stuttered at the thought of the telephone conversation to come. With a bit of luck, Scotty would take one look at the both of them and send them packing. And if it didn't happen immediately, Jimmy was sure their non-existent nursing skills would ensure that their stay north of the border would be a short one...

Suddenly his mobile phone rang, and pulling it out of his pocket, he groaned internally as the Admiral's name flashed up.

'Hello Sir,' he answered eventually, albeit reluctantly.

'Where the bloody hell are you Jimmy?' The Admiral's voice was loud enough to alert the whole carriage and several other passengers looked over at him witheringly.

'We've just left Birmingham,' Jimmy responded quietly, hoping his friend would take the hint at his lack of volume. Unfortunately, it had the opposite effect. 'Speak up man, I can't hear a bollocking word you're saying.'

'I SAID WE'VE JUST LEFT BIRMINGHAM,' Jimmy yelled, ignoring his fellow passengers in the belief that he was better irritating them now for a short period of time than risk the possibility that this conversation could last for the rest of the journey.

'I've told Hugo's offspring you're coming up today,' the Admiral went on, 'And if I say so myself, he sounded surprised. Well, speechless more like. I think he was lost for words. I patted his shoulder and told him not to worry, that getting his old man ship shape was all the thanks we needed.' Jimmy opened his mouth to interrupt, then shut it again after noting that the stares from around him were becoming more interested than irritated.

'Only one slight problem as I see it Jimmy lad,' the Admiral continued oblivious, 'We're going to have to share a coffin.' The stares were now becoming a little shocked, although Jimmy didn't know whether enlightening them to the fact that coffin was the naval slang for 'bed' would actually do him any favours...

'Old Jason's got this young bit of stuff stashed away up here,' the Admiral went on, oblivious, 'So they're a bit short on bunk space. You wait Jimmy boy, it'll be just like old times. Remember when we were hot bunking in Crete?' Jimmy cringed and closed his eyes, refusing to look around him to see what his fellow travellers thought of that little dit.

'Anyway, I can't spend all day cackling the fat with you Jimmy, I'm off to have a word with the sawbones, see when he'll let old Scotty off the hook. I'm sure when he sees how well his patient's going to be looked after, he'll be signing him off pronto...'

~*~

Florence sat on the terrace sipping a long iced Pimms. She closed her eyes in blissful enjoyment; nice and strong, just how she liked it. Okay so it wasn't necessarily the best habit to cultivate on a Tuesday lunchtime, but she'd put plenty of fruit in, so technically it counted as part of her five a day. And anyway, who knew how long she'd be here, so she might as well enjoy the little pleasures while she still had the time.

Sighing, she thought back to last night. She felt drained after her conversation with Kit. She'd put off having *the talk* for so long, it felt strange no longer having the spectre of it looming over her every action. Taking another long sip at her drink, Flo idly stroked Pepé snoozing happily on her lap.

Had she done the right thing by telling Kit her good for nothing father wasn't roasting hazelnuts in hell like he should be? She didn't know. But she did know that she couldn't leave this world only for Kit to discover that her aunt had lied to her. She might not have much time left, but Florence was determined to ensure that the person she loved most was happy and settled. She liked Jason, liked him a lot, and more importantly she thought he was perfect for Kit.

In fact, maybe a long holiday in the Highlands of Scotland was just what the doctor ordered - after she'd done what was necessary...

~*~

'My God,' Tory whispers, 'I can't believe it. It's like something out of *East Enders*. How do you feel about your dad still being alive? Do you want to see him?'

'No way.' I shake my head emphatically and purse my lips just in case she doesn't get the message. 'Why on earth would I want to go and see my father, the psychopath?'

Tory shrugs, and I know she's not buying my adamant response for a second. Thankfully, she chooses to drop the subject, or knowing my best friend, at least put it on the back burner for a minute...

'Are you going to tell Jason?'

'I'm not sure. Don't you think he's got enough on his plate without me adding my domestic problems to the mix?'

'He'd want you to tell him, you know he would,' Tory answers insistently. 'Damn it Kitty Kat, you've got to learn to let people in, let them help you. You don't have to deal with everything on your own.'

I open my mouth to argue, then shut it again. She's right, but it's not really any secret I have trust issues.

'I have to go,' I say finally, standing up, 'I've got a client meeting at ten.' Tory simply raises her eyebrows at me, knowing I'm fudging the issue. Before I can protest, her phone rings and she waves me back down again as she picks it up.

'Hey Mabel, how's it going? Have you killed him yet?' She starts to chuckle at her own joke, then her face turns serious. I sit back down.

'When did he leave? Has he said how long he intends to be gone?' There's a pause as Tory listens to Mabel's response. 'Bloody hell, he's more likely to finish Hugo off than help him get better. Don't worry I'll call him now.' Cutting the call, Tory tut tuts and asks if I've heard from Jason.

'Not since Sunday evening, why?'

'It seems like my idiotic father has taken it into his head to go up to Bloodstone Tower to, and I quote, *Nurse Hugo back to health.* Seems he thinks he might be partly responsible for his friend's stroke.' I frown in disbelief – not at the fact that the Admiral might be responsible for Hugo potentially popping his clogs, it's always a surprise to me that more people haven't exited this mortal coil due to the old bugger's interfering – but at the possibly that he might actually finally be starting to realize that his meddling can have serious consequences.

That and the fact that Jason hasn't slung him out on his ear yet.

'There's more,' Tory continues before I get a chance to express my skepticism. 'Apparently my father somehow convinced Jimmy that he should go up to play nursemaid too. He's on his way up there as we speak.'

'Oh my God, poor Jason,' I lean back into my chair feeling doubly guilty that he's having so much to deal with on his own. The reason for my beloved's lack of phone calls over the last twenty four hours is suddenly becoming crystal clear.

'Here, hold Isaac.' Tory stands up to hand me the sleeping bundle in her arms. 'I'm going to call my father now and somehow make him see bloody sense for once in his life.'

To our surprise the Admiral answers Tory's call on the second ring – not something he would usually do when his daughter's on the phone given the fact that she only ever calls him to give him a bollocking, and of course today's no different.

True to form, Tory doesn't waste any time in niceties. 'So just when did you decide that you were the reincarnation of Florence Nightingale?'

There's a pause, then a loud world weary sigh at the other end. 'A man's got to do what a man's got to do Victory.' The Admiral's tone of voice indicates an ocean of sadness at being so misunderstood and I have a hard time stopping myself from bursting out laughing. Tory rolls her eyes at me as her father continues, 'You know me Victory, it's always been a failing of mine – I'm simply too giving for my own good, always at the ready to lend a helping hand to someone in need.

'Of course I couldn't just sit by, Hugo being my friend and all.' Tory simply snorts in response to her father's description of his giving nature. 'You mean you feel bloody guilty that the balls up last summer might have had something to do with Hugo's sudden health problems.' She ignores the Admiral's huff of indignation at her bluntness, and forges on determinedly, 'So what about Jimmy? Have you dragged him halfway across the country because you think he's partly responsible for Hugo's stroke too? Or is it because he's the only person who does what you want, no questions asked?'

There's a silence on the other end of the phone and for a second I think maybe Tory's gone too far this time – not that I disagree with her – but then the Admiral surprises us both.

'You might just be right Victory,' he responds with a sigh, 'But I can't just let old Hugo fade away without giving him something worthwhile to live for.'

'And that would be you and Jimmy?' I can almost see her father nodding at the end of the phone before he answers emphatically, 'Exactly. I knew you'd understand my girl.' Tory and I exchange incredulous glances, and obviously realizing that her reasoning is so far falling deaf ears, she changes tack. 'What about Jason? How does he feel about you and Jimmy volunteering to nurse his father back to health?'

'Over the moon,' is his mindboggling answer, rendering us both momentarily speechless, 'Thought the bugger was going to kiss me at one point.' I try to imagine Jason on the verge of throwing his arms around the Admiral in an ecstasy of gratitude, but the picture firmly refuses to materialize.

'Anyway Victory, I've got to go, can't spend all my time swinging the lamp with you, I've got a patient to go and fetch.

'By the way,' he continues as Tory opens her mouth to protest, 'You might want to mention to your friend Kit that that man of hers has gone and got himself a bit of stuff stashed away, and if she's got any sense, she'll get her arse up here pretty sharpish and kick the strumpet into touch.'

And with that, the phone goes dead.

Chapter Eight

Jimmy's train finally pulled into Glasgow Central station just as the afternoon rush hour was getting ready to kick off. He was already exhausted and didn't hold out much hope of being picked up any time soon if the Admiral's cryptic, 'Sit tight Jimmy lad until you get the nod,' was anything to go by.

With a sigh he headed out of the station towards Argyle Street and the nearest pub. Might as well have a pint while he was waiting. The weather was cold, cloudy and overcast, typical of a Scottish summer, and shivering, he buttoned up his jacket as he walked towards Buchannan Street. Unfortunately the kind of old fashioned watering hole that had been so plentiful in Glasgow the last time he was here seemed to have been taken over by trendy bars with names like *Velvet Elvis* and *The Lab*, and it took him over half an hour to find something that looked reasonably promising.

Glancing up at the sign, he noted the pub's name – *O'Neill's* – he would need to tell the Admiral where he was when his old friend finally called. Then he hurried into the welcoming warmth just as it began to rain.

~*~

'I just canna stand it any longer Charlie. They're treating me like a bloody invalid. I've got to get out of here before I turn into a cabbage.'

'Thing is Scotty, they're only doing it for your own good.' The Admiral's response was lame at best and drew a derisory snort

60

from the figure on the bed.

They'd been waiting for over an hour for the consultant to do his rounds and Hugo was becoming increasingly irate at the thought of spending another day in the small cupboard that passed as a private hospital room. The Admiral decided it was time to play his ace in the hole.

'Scotty, you don't need to fret any longer. You won't be stopping in this mausoleum for another night. I was keeping this as a surprise, but I can't sit and watch you hauling on a fouled anchor for another second.' He beamed at his bewildered friend before delivering the punch line. 'Me and Jimmy are going to take care of you. We're going to stay at the Tower until you get back on your feet. Now I'm sure when the doctor realizes how well you'll be looked after, he'll let you out straight away.'

Hugo stared at his prospective *nurse* with something approaching horror. He appeared completely lost for words. It certainly wasn't the response the Admiral had expected, and to be honest he felt a little miffed.

'Well, we might be a bit rusty on the old bed pan etiquette Scotty, but I must confess I was expecting a bit more bloody gratitude than you're showing at the moment.'

Hugo visibly gathered himself together and made a concerted effort to look grateful. 'I'm sorry Charlie, I know you want to help but the truth is... well, you know the *Invincible* reunion down in Pompey on Friday...?' The Admiral frowned and butted in, 'Load of bollocking old wind bags getting together to talk about the good old days? Of course I know about it. You wouldn't catch me within a hundred miles of a bloody cake and arse party like that. Wouldn't have thought it'd be your cup o' tea either Scotty.'

Hugo coughed and looked sheepish. 'Well, the thing is Charlie...' He paused, causing the Admiral to narrow his eyes in suspicion, before continuing in a rush, 'The thing is, I've arranged to meet Alice Winterbottom, you know that wren I went out with while we were at Collingwood?'

There was a short silence while the Admiral assimilated this startling piece of news. Finally he gave a bark of laughter and shook his head. 'Old Chilly Arse – how could I forget her? Bloody hell Scotty, you dark horse, I didn't think you had it in you.'

Hugo shook his head sadly before saying gloomily, 'If he finds out about it, there's no way Jason'll let me go. He'll have me tucked up in bed with a cup of hot chocolate for the rest of my bloody natural if he has his way.'

There was another silence while both men contemplated the horrors of getting old and subject to the whims of well meaning offspring. Then suddenly the Admiral jumped up and hurried to the open door. Hugo watched in bewilderment as his friend stuck his head through the opening, looked up and down the passageway outside, before closing the door, locking it quickly and turning back to Hugo.

'Right Scotty, get your stuff together, we're breaking you out. There's no way you're going to miss the opportunity to have a last bonk before you pop your clogs...'

~*~

'What the hell does he mean, a bit of stuff stashed away? Do you think Jason's having an affair?'

'I'd hardly think he's had the time,' is Tory's matter of fact response, 'My father's no doubt got his wires crossed – let's be honest, it wouldn't be the first time. If I were you, I'd pay absolutely no attention whatsoever.'

I frown, trying to remember if Jason had mentioned anyone new in our last conversation.

'I thought you had a meeting at ten?' Tory's question cuts into my reverie, and glancing down at my watch, I mouth, 'Shit,' before jumping up to grab my things and running for the front door. I have fifteen minutes to get to my appointment on the other side of the river. 'I'll call you as soon as I get home,' I shout at the same time as trying to find my prospective client's address on my phone and locate my car keys...

In the end it takes me over twenty minutes to get to my appointment, and as I park up, all thoughts of possible cheating partners go right out of my head as I walk up the path to the front door – mainly because I'm too busy staring at a large coffin sitting in the front garden with its lid propped at a jaunty angle next to it. I stop dead (pardon the pun), then, heart thumping, I tiptoe towards the tomb wondering what the bloody hell I'm going to do if there's someone in it...

...There isn't. In fact it appears to be filled with newly planted petunias and there's a small brass plaque placed strategically on the open lid with the words, *Donna and Norman live here.*

With more than a little trepidation, I ring the door bell. After a couple of minutes, a small, slightly rotund, blond woman answers the door. I stare mutely at her for a couple of seconds, taking in the head to toe black, complete with pure white pancake makeup covering her face and chest, finished off with beautifully painted blood red lips.

'Err...Donna?' I say faintly, pulling myself together with effort. She nods her head sorrowfully, and getting back into my stride, I show her my card, and apologize profusely for being late. At which point she promptly bursts into tears...

I open my mouth before realizing I have no idea what to say. Still sobbing quietly, she ushers me into a small sitting room and goes off to make us both a cup of tea. I sit frozen for a few seconds and I'm ashamed to admit I actually think about legging it while she's otherwise occupied.

Fortunately the room seems almost incongruously normal with its flowery chintz curtains and magnolia wallpaper, and of course, at the end of the day, I don't want to be responsible for adding to her woes. So I reluctantly abandon the idea of making a run for it and instead pull my portfolio out for her to have a look at. Hopefully once she's seen what I'm capable of, she'll buck up (obviously I won't be showing her the chocolate penises...)

After about ten minutes by which time I'm beginning to get seriously worried, she finally reappears with the tea. Although she's stopped crying, her face is blotchy and the red lipstick has migrated down her chin and just under her nose, making her look like a mad clown. Fighting the urge to re-think my earlier decision not to leg it, I struggle to keep my face neutral and sip my tea, waiting for her to explain.

'The thing is, we thought it was all sorted,' she hiccupped, handing me a Jammy Dodger, 'She seemed so nice.'

'Err, who seemed nice?' I butt in, anxious to be kept in the loop.

'The wedding planner. We got her out of *'Tales From The Crypt'* magazine. Said she specialized in unusual locations.'

'So where is she?' I ask while internally thinking, 'Tales from the crypt – WTF?' Out loud I continue politely, 'And what kind of unusual location are we talking about?'

'Everything was fine until we paid her the money up front, then she did a runner, leaving us high and dry.' I shake my head sympathetically. There are so many charlatans in event organizing nowadays.

'So… the unusual location…?' I prompt.

'We lost Rupert last year,' she murmurs, giving a small pathetic sniff, prompting me to pat her knee comfortingly. 'He'd been our best friend for over fifteen years. We simply couldn't imagine having the wedding without him.

'And of course, given Norman's fondness for the macabre, we thought it was perfect.' I stare at her completely nonplussed, so after pausing for a second, she continues, 'And there's a nice abandoned crypt nearby which we've been allowed to use for the wedding breakfast.'

'A crypt?' I ask faintly.

'Yes, near to the cemetery,' she responds with her first smile, 'Where we're holding the ceremony. Just by Rupert's grave. He'd be so pleased.'

As I head back to my flat I fight the urge to bang my head on the steering wheel. What on earth was I thinking? The thing is, I've always been a sucker for a sob story, especially when someone has been cheated. So here I am, having promised to finish organizing the wedding of Dartmouth's answer to the Adams Family, which is due to take place in a half derelict crypt, in just under a week's time. No pressure…

~*~

In the end Hugo's big break out was a bit of damp squib and the Admiral had to admit (if only privately) that he was a little disappointed. He'd always fancied jumping into a getaway car and taking off with a squeal of tires and burning exhaust. Instead, no one challenged them as they made their way laboriously down to the main entrance, and it took another ten minutes while they rummaged round in various pockets to come up with enough change for the car park.

By the time they were both ensconced in the Admiral's aging Vauxhall, Hugo was looking worryingly pale, and for the first time the Admiral wondered whether this whole bucket list thing was actually a good idea. What they needed was somewhere to hole up and plan their strategy.

But first, he had to go back to Bloodstone Tower to pick up Pickles. Of course, this might prove a bit tricky given the fact that they needed to keep a low profile and anyone copping an eye on them would bugger things up completely, but leaving without the elderly spaniel was unthinkable.

As the Admiral drove slowly out of the hospital main gates, he was a little concerned that he hadn't really thought this escape plan through, but then improvisation was his middle name and had gotten him out of many a sticky situation over the years. As they drove out of Glasgow, he felt his spirits lift a little. It was time to call Jimmy.

Thanks to Victory he had something called *Blue Teeth* in his car. His daughter had insisted he get it fitted when he'd ended up in the Escape Lane after trying to find his mobile phone in the pocket of his trousers while coming down Telegraph Hill on the A38. Of course the whole bloody shenanigans hadn't been his fault, but he had to admit having this contraption in his car was damn useful.

'CALL JIMMY NOON,' he yelled abruptly causing Hugo to almost jump out of his seat. The Admiral turned to his friend and grinned as the shrill ringing tone sounded through the car. 'Technology, eh Scotty?'

'Hello, is that you Sir?' Jimmy's voice over the speaker sounded small and anxious.

'WHAT IS YOUR LOCATION?' The Admiral bellowed, getting caught up in the excitement of his first clandestine operation in years.

'I'M IN A PUB,' yelled back Jimmy automatically. The sound of his voice reverberating round the car was so loud, the Admiral only narrowly missed an oncoming truck as he swerved automatically.

'BLOODY HELL JIMMY KEEP IT DOWN WILL YOU, WE'RE IN A CAR, NOT A BOLLOCKING AIRCRAFT HANGER,' Charles Shackleford continued, totally oblivious to the fact that his voice was loud enough to wake the dead. 'I'VE GOT SCOTTY. SPRUNG HIM FROM THE HOSPITAL HALF AN HOUR AGO. WE ARE CONDUCTING *OPERATION RESCUE PICKLES* THEN WE'LL RENDEZVOUS AT YOUR CURRENT LOCATION. DO NOT MOVE FROM YOUR PRESENT POSITION, I REPEAT, DO NOT MOVE FROM YOUR PRESENT POSITION. OVER AND OUT.'

Consumed with excitement, the Admiral cut the call with a flourish and screeched to a halt to avoid an old lady attempting to cross the road at a pedestrian crossing. 'Bloody hell, that was close. I don't know what's wrong with people nowadays, they just don't pay attention to things.

'It was different in our day. We never missed a trick did we Scotty? Sharp as bloody needles, that was us. We knew what was important. We could sift through mountains of information and instinctively know exactly which bit was vital...'

'You mean like exactly where Jimmy's current location actually is?' Hugo butted in drily, holding onto the dashboard for dear life.

'Exactly,' the Admiral responded, completely oblivious to his friend's sarcasm. 'We've still got it Scotty, we're still on the ball. You wait and see, this is going to be a road trip you'll never forget. We'll call it *Operation Leg Over*. What do you say?'

~*~

As soon as I get back to my flat, I pour myself a large glass of wine. Why oh why did I agree to help? Sinking down onto my sofa, I take a long gulp and pull out my notes.

After a quick look through, I begin to feel a little better. To be honest, the whole thing shouldn't be too difficult to finalize. Luckily my predecessor had already taken care of most of the details before she did a bunk. The whole service at the cemetery bit appears to have been sorted pretty much completely. Can't imagine what the registrar conducting the ceremony will be thinking. Still, not my problem. It's the wedding breakfast at the abandoned crypt I need to focus on. If I can get this one right, I can do anything...

~*~

Everything seemed quiet as they pulled up outside Hugo's home. To the Admiral's relief, Jason's car was nowhere to be seen, but just to be on the safe side, he parked the Vauxhall in a small hidden grassy area halfway up the driveway. 'Now you stay put Scotty. I'm not going to pick you up any smalls, thought we could grab you some on the way – no sense in hanging around and asking for trouble.' Scotty nodded his head before frowning and saying abruptly, 'Ma uniform, I've got to get ma uniform – they'll nae let me into the Mess otherwise.'

'Bugger it,' the Admiral muttered, 'This operation is getting more complicated by the bollocking second.' He sat thinking for a moment, and as he did so, they were alerted by a sudden noise. Glancing in the rear-view mirror, the Admiral stage whispered, 'Hide,' just as Jason's car drove passed them towards the house. Both men dove for the floor thinking the game was surely up. However, when nothing happened after a couple of minutes, they breathed a sigh of relief and went to sit up straight – or rather Hugo did, the Admiral was unfortunately stuck with his head under the wheel.

'How the bloody hell did ye get your head in there?' Hugo asked incredulously. His friend didn't answer – mainly because his vocal cords were blocked by his double chin.

'Hang on a second Charlie, I'll get ye out o' there in a jiffy.' Hurriedly opening his door, Hugo clambered out as the Admiral started mumbling something that sounded like, 'Nth, nth, nth…'

Creeping round the back of the car, Hugo looked furtively up the driveway to see if there was any movement. When he was satisfied his son wasn't on his way back, he hastily pulled open the Admiral's door, only to be faced with the large expanse of his friend's nether regions. 'Did ye know yer arse is hanging out those trousers Charlie boy? Ye need to go on a bloody diet.'

'Nth, nth, nth…'

'I think the best way to free ye will be to try and pull the seat back. Hold yer horses while I find the handle.' Bending down, Hugo shoved his hand in between the seat and the Admiral's head, trying to find a lever to pull. When the first thing he managed to yank elicited a muffled yell from the Admiral, he mumbled sorry and reached out further, eventually finding the handle to slide the seat back.

Finally, with a loud clunking noise, the chair shifted, freeing the Admiral's head which shot up like a Jack in a Box. 'What a load of bloody horlicks,' he wheezed after he'd recovered sufficiently to regain his voice.

'What are we going to do now Charlie?' Hugo whispered urgently, 'Ye canna go get ma gear now Jason's back. He'll surely know yer up to something. The lad's uncannily observant.' The Admiral narrowed his eyes, acknowledging that he might be up against someone who could be as devious as himself when the need called for it. But then again, he'd never yet met anyone he couldn't outsmart in an emergency.

'Right,' he said decisively, 'We'll sit here and wait until it's dark – there's more chance of everyone being in bed then.'

'But, but, we canna wait that long Charlie, they'll be out looking for us. And what about Jimmy?'

'They'll never suspect we'd be daft enough to come back here, and don't you worry about Jimmy, he can get us a room in Glasgow – that'll give us time to plan our next move.

'In the meantime, try and get a bit of shut eye Scotty old man, you're going to need all your strength for your assignation with old Alice...'

Chapter Nine

Donna has made it quite clear, that she wants the crypt to be decorated as a gothic masterpiece – the spookier the better, complete with cobwebs and bats (fake preferably). Oh, and apparently everyone is dressing up too…

Okay, so spooky crypt equals Halloween. Have you ever tried to get Halloween decorations at the end of June – especially when they're needed urgently? I've been trawling the internet for hours and so far all I've managed to come up with is a job lot of plastic fangs (complete with bloody teeth) left over from last year. Still, they should make the tables look nice and festive…

I haven't been over to check out said crypt yet – strangely enough I thought I'd leave that until daylight. My predecessor has at least taken care of the nuts and bolts in the form of port-aloos and a bar, but so far there are no tables or chairs ordered, no tablecloths, crockery, cutlery, disco, decorations, or (more importantly) a cleaner. The food, I've been reliably informed by the bride, is being done by the groom's mother and his two sisters. I think I'll just check they have everything in hand then leave them to it.

The chairs for the ceremony are being transported to the cemetery by someone from a local funeral parlour - I daren't ask which one - so all we need up there is some black ribbon. Come to think of it, black ribbon might be the answer to all my problems, and not just black, I'll use red too.

Perfect - blood and darkness – what could be more gothic? And candles, lots and lots of candles.

You know what? I think I'm getting into the swing of things – mmmwwwwahahahahaha (see, I can do an evil laugh too...) Sod the bats, they're just going to have to live without them. And as for cobwebs, we'll no doubt have our very own, so when I book the cleaners, I'll just tell them to leave a few in the corners.

That reminds me, I'd better get the bride and groom to sign a disclaimer, just in case they set the place on fire...

Yes, things are shaping up very nicely.

I'm just about to place an order for enough ribbon to decorate the whole of Dracula's castle when my phone rings. I glance down and my heart flips. It's Jason. As I take the call, I can't stem the tide of longing that swamps me. 'Hey sweetheart, how's it going? It's so good to hear your voice,' I murmur, wishing he was here in person so I could show him just how much I'm missing him. Unfortunately, his response throws a whole bucketful of freezing cold water on any lustful thoughts I might have.

'About as bad as it can be.' His voice is abrupt, tight with anger and worry. 'My father's gone from the hospital. Charles bloody Shackleford kidnapped him from his room this afternoon.'

~*~

By eleven o'clock, it was as dark as it was going to get. The strange twilight cast tortured shadows around the car and everything was silent. There were no lights visible through the trees, giving a good indication that the residents of Bloodstone Tower were in bed. Charles Shackleford suppressed his excitement. Phase two of *Operation Leg Over* was about to commence. He'd managed to get a couple of hours sleep, and now he was ready to go.

'This is the life,' he thought gleefully, 'Surviving on a few hours sleep snatched here and there in between risking life and limb on dangerous assignments.' Excitedly he leaned over to wake his sleeping friend. 'Come on Scotty old man, time to wake up.' Then, climbing laboriously out of the Vauxhall, he stuck his head back in, patted Hugo on the shoulder and pointed to the seat he'd just vacated. 'Get yourself in there Scotty and turn the car round. You need to be ready to go as soon as I get back with Pickles and your gear. Leave the rest to me...'

It took the Admiral over ten minutes to negotiate the dark lane up to the Tower. He'd forgotten how bloody creepy this place was at night and every rustle in the bushes nearly had him hightailing it back to the car, dangerous assignments be buggered. He held his nerve however and eventually managed to sneak round to the kitchen.

Using Hugo's key, he unlocked and opened the kitchen door wide enough to poke his head through. After waiting a few seconds, satisfied there was no one there, he gingerly stepped inside before turning back to close the door quietly behind him. He was just putting the key back in his pocket when out of the corner of his eye he spied a large shape looming out of the darkness. Heart in his mouth, he had time to mumble, 'Wha' the boll...' before the shape was on him and he head butted the closed door with a resounding thump which shook the frame. Thinking he was surely doomed, the Admiral could swear his life began to flash before him, until suddenly a large wet tongue was stuck in his ear. Pickles.

Almost weak with relief, the Admiral pushed the dog off with a whispered, 'Get down you daft dog. What'r you trying to do – give me a bollocking heart attack? At this rate I'll be pushing up the bloody daisies before old Scotty.' Pickles' response was to simply whimper ecstatically and the Admiral decided it would be best to let his furry companion calm down a bit before executing the next stage in his plan, especially as he wasn't entirely sure where Scotty's bedroom was.

It took about ten minutes before Pickles settled down enough for the Admiral to order the spaniel into his basket, and after a whispered, 'Stay,' he took a deep breath and tiptoed in the direction of the Great Hall.

Five tortuous minutes later he'd made it up to the first floor landing. By now he was having second thoughts about the whole risking life and limb thing. His heart was hammering so hard in his chest, he was almost convinced it was giving up the ghost.

He stopped for a second to get his bearings and wait for his eyes to adjust in the pitch black. It was all very well sneaking around in the middle of the night, but the last time he'd done it had been forty odd years ago. Briefly Charles Shackleford thought back to the memorable fiasco in Bangkok, before finally admitting to himself that he might actually be a tad old for this cloak and dagger stuff. Still, it was no good ball aching at this late stage.

Sighing, he brought his mind back to the matter at hand. Hugo said his bedroom was at the end of the hall, opposite the bathroom. Stealthily he crept along the dark passageway, until he came to the last door. As quietly as possible he eased it open and breathed a sigh of relief when he saw it was empty. In the moonlight, he could see Scotty's Mess Kit laid neatly on the bed. Thanking his lucky stars that he didn't have to go rummaging around for his friend's gear, the Admiral tiptoed over to the bed and went to pick up the uniform. It weighed a ton. 'Bollocks,' he groaned, there was no way he was going to be able to get back down the stairs carrying this lot. There was only one thing for it, he was going to have to put the bloody thing on.

It took him nearly twenty minutes to struggle into his friend's Mess Kit – unfortunately Hugo was considerably smaller - and by the time the Admiral had squeezed himself into the waistcoat and jacket, he was puffing and panting, not to mention sweating profusely.

He hadn't been able to do up any of the buttons on the dress shirt or waistcoat, and glancing down at himself, the Admiral could only be thankful he was wearing a vest. Wheezing, he sat back on the bed for a quick breather. He just had to get the trousers on now and he'd be done.

After a couple of minutes, he felt recovered enough to give it a go. Then he had a sudden thought. It really would be better if he went to the toilet before struggling into Scotty's dress pants, and the bathroom was just across the hall.

Emboldened by his success so far, the Admiral decided he had enough time to have a quick pee, then once his bladder was back in business, it would be easy enough to put the trousers on in the bathroom. In the meantime he hung them round his neck by the braces leaving his hands free to carry his own clothes. Finally, he squashed his feet into Scotty's shoes and headed to the bedroom door in his underpants.

Before stepping out onto the landing, he paused for a second to listen. Then, satisfied he hadn't been rumbled, he scuttled over to the bathroom and quickly pushed open the door.

The scream was blood curdling, not to mention loud enough to wake the residents of every cemetery within a five mile radius. The Admiral stared for one horrified second at the elderly woman sitting on the toilet in front of him, before looking down at his naked hairy legs sticking out the bottom of Hugo's dress shirt. Then he dropped his bundle of clothes and ran.

His sprint down the stairs would have given Usain Bolt a run for his money and he reached the kitchen in record time. Still in his basket, the Springer spaniel wagged his tail uncertainly as his master dashed past, threw open the back door and staggered through.

'COME ON PICKLES GET YOUR ARSE IN GEAR,' the Admiral yelled, completely abandoning any attempt at stealth, before blundering through the undergrowth in the general direction of the car.

Hugo was sitting anxiously at the wheel of the Vauxhall, engine on ready, when he heard sudden shouting and barking getting gradually louder. Glancing in the rear-view mirror, he stared incredulously as the figure of the Admiral burst through the bushes.

For some reason his friend wasn't wearing any trousers but instead had them hanging around his neck where they were flapping behind his head, giving him the appearance of a demented Batman.

The Admiral lurched towards him with Pickles in tow, bellowing, 'GO, GO, GO,' as he shoved the spaniel into the back and threw himself in the passenger seat.

In a manoeuvre worthy of James Bond at his best, Hugo stamped his foot down on the accelerator pedal and they skidded off the grass on to the drive, before taking off in a squeal of brakes and scorched exhaust, exactly as the Admiral had so longed for earlier.

~*~

As a council of war goes, it has to be said, ours isn't very impressive. Basically me, Tory, Freddy, Mabel, Emily, and of course little Isaac. As it's only nine am, Dotty has decided that councils of war are beneath her, so she's still in bed (and of course the biscuits haven't been unwrapped yet.) We're sitting in Tory's kitchen deciding on a course of action which doesn't involve all of us scouring the whole country searching for three daft old men and a dog.

'Exactly what time did Jason say my father left the hospital with Hugo?' Tory's trying to put together some kind of time line in an effort to track the movements of our three fugitives.

'The car park CCTV shows them driving out at around two thirty. I think they may be...' My theory is cut short (which is probably a good thing, it wasn't much of a theory) as my mobile phone starts ringing. 'It's Jason,' I say, swiping the front hurriedly. 'Have you found them yet?' I ask before he has chance to speak.

'Not yet, but the plot is certainly getting thicker,' he replies, 'Would you believe the Admiral sneaked into the Tower last night. I think he'd come to fetch his dog and probably grab my father some more clothes. He would have got away without anyone being the wiser had he not decided to use the bathroom before he left.'

'You heard him then?' I butt in excitedly – I can't help it, the whole thing's a bit like a BBC drama.

'I think they heard him across the loch,' Jason responded drily, 'He surprised my grandmother on the toilet. Apparently he wasn't wearing any trousers. Needless to say she's taken to her bed with a bottle of smelling salts.'

'That's awful,' I say doing my damndest not to laugh. 'Why on earth wasn't he wearing any trousers?'

'This is Charles Shackleford we're talking about. Who knows why the bloody man does anything? Anyway, we think my father was waiting for the Admiral in the car, so that pretty much rules out the possibility that he was there against his will. I have no idea where they are now.'

'How about Jimmy, do you think he was with them?'

'No sign of him at the hospital. Have you spoken to Emily?'

'Emily and Mabel are here now,' I answer. 'They've tried calling but, surprise, surprise, nobody's answering.'

'I'm having no luck with my father either.' Jason sighs and I can hear the concern in his voice. 'I know he's an adult and perfectly entitled to leave hospital if he wishes, but I'm worried about him Kit. His health's not good. He should be resting, not gallivanting round the damn country.'

'Try not to worry too much,' I say softly, wanting nothing more than to put my arms around him. 'We'll keep trying to contact them from here. Let's keep each other informed. I'm sure they'll get in touch soon. And if nobody's heard from them by the end of today,' I add impulsively, 'I'll come up to Scotland tomorrow.'

Even as the words are tripping off my tongue, my brain is shouting, 'No, no, no, you idiot, you have the bloody Bride of Dracula's wedding in three days time.' Damn it, what have I done? I hold my breath, hoping he'll tell me it's not necessary, but instead the relief in his voice makes me feel worse. 'I'd really like that, if you think you can spare the time.'

'Of course I can,' I respond lightly, feeling slightly sick.

'I thought you said you've got a bit of a shot gun wedding to arrange?' Freddy asks when I finally put down the phone. As usual, he doesn't miss a trick. I open my mouth to answer but Tory gets there first.

'Well if you're going up to Scotland, then I'm coming with you.'

'Me too,' Mabel adds in a whisper, looking as though she's about to cry.

'And if you think you're going looking for my husband without me, then you've got another think coming.' Emily's voice in contrast is brusque, giving no room for argument. I can't help but feel a little sorry for Jimmy when she finds him...

An hour later both Mabel and Emily leave to start packing. I try to explain that we might not be going, but it's like water off a duck's back. The best I can do is to make them promise to let us know if their husbands get in touch in the meantime.

'We can't all get in my little Fiesta,' I say irritably to Tory as soon as the front door shuts behind them, 'Especially not with Isaac's car seat in there too, not to mention Dotty, who I presume will be along for the ride. And anyway, isn't Noah supposed to be coming back tomorrow?'

Tory ignores my grouchiness, answering blithely, 'We'll go in my car and Noah can meet us up there.'

'I can't,' I wail suddenly, the feeling of impending doom swamping me for a second, 'I have a wedding to organize in three days time. And not just any wedding, this one's in a bloody cemetery. I can't just up and leave.'

'So why did you say you'd go then?' Freddy asks matter of factly, reaching for a biscuit, 'And why are they having a wedding in a cemetery?'

Chapter Ten

The Admiral could tell Jimmy wasn't totally on board with his cunning plan. For the most part he looked as though he couldn't decide whether to throw himself on the mercy of his wife, or simply throw himself out of the window.

'You can't call Emily,' the Admiral explained for the umpteenth time, 'If you do, she'll know where we're going. I hate to say it Jimmy boy, but you always were a bit of a gatling gob and there's no way you'd be able to keep that little gem from the dragon.'

They were sitting in a motorway services just south of the border between Scotland and England. They'd left their hotel room in Glasgow a couple of hours ago after polishing off a hearty breakfast – or rather his had been pretty hearty – actually bordering on coronary fodder if he was being honest – but the other two had simply picked at theirs, with Jimmy actually ordering muesli – *muesli* for God's sake. What kind of breakfast is that for a man?

The Admiral wasn't sure if old Scotty was off his food due to excitement about his upcoming assignation with Alice, or if he was just off his food. Either way, he'd just nibbled at a slice of toast in the hotel restaurant and the Admiral was concerned. It was up to him to ensure that the Scotsman had plenty of fuel inside him to prepare him for his upcoming night of passion – otherwise the Admiral was actually worried that his friend might not survive it.

So this time he'd piled up Hugo's plate with some good old fashioned fish and chips. And to be fair, the Scot did seem to be enjoying it much more than his pathetic slice of toast this morning.

'Now Scotty, how long do you think we've got before that son of yours discovers your Mess Kit's missing?' Hugo frowned, thinking. 'Well I got them out of the wardrobe to check for moths, then left them on the bed to air. If he'd noticed them, he'd have said something. Jason dinna mince words as you know. That's why I didnae tell him about the reunion – he'd have put a stop to it for sure.' The Admiral nodded slowly. 'So, we can safely assume he doesn't know we're on our way down to Pompey.'

'How were you going to get there Scotty?' Jimmy interrupted, taking a bite out of his sandwich, which the Admiral noted with a shudder actually had *lettuce* in it. 'You know, before you had your err funny turn?' the small man continued, not wanting to mention the word stroke in case it upset his friend. Hugo didn't seem to notice.

'There's a coach leaving Glasgow at lunchtime today. We were to be staying overnight in a Travelodge in Birmingham, then going onto Pompey tomorrow. The dinner 's due to start at nineteen hundred, but I told Alice I'd meet her in the Wardroom bar at eighteen hundred – you know to get reacquainted like.'

Hugo's face turned a bright shade of red as he said the word *reacquainted* which the Admiral thought was a bit excessive seeing as he didn't think the Scot included giving Alice a quick one over the coffee table in his understanding of the word...

'Right then,' he said with satisfaction, 'We're going to be ahead of the game Scotty. You'll be in Pompey by lunchtime tomorrow so you'll have plenty of time to spruce yourself up a bit. As long as young Captain Buchannan doesn't cotton on to the fact that your uniform's done a runner, we'll be in the clear until you give him a call the day after tomorrow.'

'I think I could well be divorced by then,' Jimmy offered despondently.

The Admiral tutted impatiently. 'Don't be such a bloody poodle faker Jimmy boy, That woman has you by the short and curlies. You need to show her who's boss once in a while. If you ask me, you're eating far too much bunny grub – it's turning you into a damn wimp.'

'Well what about Mabel?' Jimmy responded, stung at the Admiral's assessment of his marriage. 'I don't think she's going to very happy with you either Sir.'

'You leave Mabel to me,' his friend responded airily, 'Got her round my little finger – the woman's like putty in my hand.'

'Didn't look much like putty when she threatened to shoot you for stepping on the floor she'd just mopped,' Jimmy was quick to point out, causing Hugo to snigger a bit - which he swiftly turned into a cough when the Admiral turned to glare at him.

'And I think you've forgotten about one other person Sir,' Jimmy went on knowingly. 'It's very likely that Tory's going to have your balls for breakfast when she finally catches up with you...'

~*~

'It's no good, if I'm not back in time, you're going to have to do it.'

It's not often I see Freddy lost for words and I have to fight the urge to take a photo.

I've spent the whole day making sure that everything is up to speed with Dracula's wedding, and all that remains now is to deal with the actual day itself.

'I mean, I'm sure I *will* be back, but just in case I'm not, you'll have to take over.'

'No bloody chance,' Freddy finally splutters coming out of his horrified trance. 'There's no way I'm supervising a bloody wedding in a cemetery followed by The Rocky Horror Show in a crypt. I think you're barking mad to have taken it on in the first place with everything you've got going on.'

'Oh come on Freddy,' I wheedle, 'I know you're off this weekend and Jacques is still in America. Just think how you love to dress up. This will be an amazing opportunity to go to town. Bela Lugosi's got nothing on you, and I'm sure you've got all the props you need in your theatre storeroom.'

'No.'

'I really need you to do this for me Freddy.'

'No.'

'It's really important to me Freddy. You're my best friend, who else can I ask?'

'No.'

'I'll make it up to you I promise, and I'll never forget what you've done for me.'

'No.'

'If you care about me at all, you'll do this for me.'

'No.'

'If you don't agree to do it, I'll tell Jacques about the Flamenco dancer.'

'You wouldn't.'

'Try me.'

'You're a complete bitch Kit Davies. You are so going to owe me – BIG TIME. And if it all goes tits up then it's your funeral.'

'Funeral, I like it,' pipes up Tory who's so far stayed right out of the conversation.

'Have you spoken to Noah yet?' I ask her, thinking now it a perfect time to change the subject. After all, Freddy might not have to take over yet. The Three Amigos could well be home and tucked up in bed with a cup of cocoa and a thick ear...

'Yep, he thinks it's all a bit of a hoot. We had a fairly long conversation about responsibilities and now we're not speaking.'

'Oh no, Tory, that's awful,' I stammer thinking back to the time they broke up last summer. She chuckles at the look on my face. 'Don't worry Kitty Kat, I'll let him take me and Isaac away for a sumptuous weekend of rich food, carnal delights and nappy changing. It'll do him good.'

I breathe a sigh of relief that their spat was nothing serious.

'If we do end up going tomorrow, then he'll get a flight to Glasgow and meet us there.'

'What if they're not in Scotland?' Freddy asks, obviously still miffed at being out manoeuvred.

'Where else could they be?' I ask, 'It's not as if they're likely to drive down to the South coast is it? I mean as far as we know, they're in the Admiral's car and we all know what a heap of junk that is. I'm sure Tory's father wouldn't risk driving it back on a long trip south so soon after taking it all that way north...'

~*~

'Now what are we going to do?' Hugo murmured despondently, all thoughts of his upcoming night of debauchery going up in smoke along with the smouldering remains of what had been the Admiral's Vauxhall engine.

As the three men stood staring glumly, Charles Shackleford had to admit - if only privately – that it might have been the squeal of tires and burning exhaust of their getaway that put the final nail in the coffin.

They'd made it as far as Stafford before the Vauxhall had given up the ghost with a puff of smoke and a loud bang, and now they were stranded on the hard shoulder of the M6.

'I'm in the AA,' offered Jimmy after no one else had come up with any ideas. 'I could give them a call.' He rummaged around for his wallet and brought out a battered orange card. 'Oh no, it's got Emily's name on the front.' He looked up. 'Should I call her?' he continued hopefully.

'Definitely not,' the Admiral declared vehemently, 'She'll have everyone and his dog on our tail as soon as she puts down the phone. And talking about dogs, come here Pickles, we'll go for a quick walk while I think about our next move.'

'You can't go for a walk on the motorway Sir,' Jimmy protested as the Admiral tugged on Pickles' leash. Judging by his reluctance, it was clear the elderly spaniel agreed with him. The other two watched in disbelief as the Admiral started towing the Springer along the hard shoulder.

'HAVE EITHER OF YOU GOT ANY POO BAGS?' he yelled back a couple of minutes later, then, 'NO, HOLD YOUR POSITION, I'VE GOT A PACKET OF MINT IMPERIALS SO I'LL USE THAT.'

Jimmy and Hugo sat on the grassy bank next to the car and watched the large man become smaller and smaller until he disappeared over a hill in the distance. He didn't seem to notice the cars whizzing past him.

'Do you think he'll come back?' Jimmy asked at length.

'Aye, if he doesnae get bloody run over first, the daft sod,' responded Hugo, shaking his head.

They sat in silence for a few more minutes, looking anxiously to their right, then suddenly a lorry coming towards them put on its indicator light and began slowing down. The two men stood up, initially concerned that the van might actually plough into their only means of transport, but as it got closer they could see their friend in the passenger seat with Pickles sat on his knee. The lorry stopped a few feet away from the Vauxhall and the Admiral opened the door and leaned out. 'Grab the gear and hop in gentlemen, we've got ourselves a lift to Birmingham.'

The cabin was admittedly squashed with all three of them perched up next to the driver who turned out to be a Brummie who'd served twenty years in the Royal Navy.

'Colin here has offered to take us all the way to that Travelodge your coach is stopping at Scotty. I thought we could wait for it to arrive, then sneak on board and act like we got on it in Glasgow. Most of the ship mates on it are likely so bloody ancient, they wouldn't know whether we'd been there or not. We know there's at least one free seat, and a couple of the old buggers are bound to get themselves lost before we get to Pompey.

'Anyone want a mint?...'

~*~

It's nine o'clock in the evening and there's been no sign of our three missing geriatrics.

Now I've made sure I've got everything covered for The Bride of Frankenstein just in case I don't make it back in three days, I feel actually pretty excited at the prospect of seeing Jason again tomorrow. I'm actually really surprised how much I've missed him, and while I'm still far from convinced that missing some-body is grounds for uprooting one's entire life and relocating five hundred miles away in the middle of nowhere, I'm definitely warming to the idea.

Tory is going to pick up Mabel and Emily as soon as she's fed Isaac (who doubles up as our synchronized watch), and once she gives me the green light, I'll get the passenger ferry over to Kingswear and meet them.

Tory and I will take turns at driving – all a bit déjà vu-ish to be honest. We'll pick Noah up at Glasgow airport on the way and hopefully arrive at Bloodstone Tower in time for supper.

I've written Freddy a complete list of absolutely everything he has to do, along with a timeline spelling out exactly what time he has to do it. Should be a piece of cake really – I'm not sure what all the fuss is about. Sometimes Freddy can be such a drama queen. Still, I opt for sending an email instead of phoning on the grounds that it's a bit late...

I just have one thing left to do, and that's to phone Aunt Flo to update her on the exciting events of the last twenty four hours. If I know her, she'll be taking down notes to use in her next book. Smiling, I dial her number, but it goes straight to voice mail. Did she say she was going out this evening?

Obviously I'm not her keeper, but she usually lets me know if she's doing something. I glance down at my own answer phone and notice the flashing red light for the first time. Hurriedly pressing the play button, I'm surprised at my relief as my aunt's dry tones float up.

'Kit darling, I'm going to stay in London for a few days with Neil, and I'm taking Pepé with me. It's a spur of the moment decision and Neil's promised to take me to see that wonderful ex-hibition of the Queen's dresses at the Palace. I shouldn't be away much longer than a week, but it's a chance for me to do some re-search for my next book at the V&A. I'll call you when I get back. Take care sweetie.'

I debate whether to try her mobile, but then she never answers it anyway. The message was left at ten this morning. She'll be with Neil by now and I'm sure he'll phone me if she does an Agatha Christie and disappears under mysterious circumstances. I decide to leave my aunt to her few days away. She and Neil don't get to spend too much time together so it will do them both good, and I'll no doubt have a tale to tell her when she's gets back...

~*~

The Admiral, Jimmy and Hugo were sitting in the bar at the Travelodge, furtively spying on the group of elderly gentlemen tottering into the reception.

Colin the Brummie lorry driver had dropped the three of them off a couple of hours before the coach had pulled into the car park, so they'd had a bit of time to plan how they were going to integrate themselves into the group.

'How many are there?' the Admiral asked in a loud whisper, 'Bloody hell, some of them look over ninety. Do you recognize any of them Scotty?'

Hugo gave each man a surreptitious once over. 'Nae met any o' them before. Ma old shipmates mostly live down in your neck of the woods Charlie, so we're meeting up at the dinner.' The Admiral nodded in satisfaction. 'Toppers, we're not likely to get rumbled then.'

He turned back to his two friends. 'Right this is what we'll do. We'll hang around here until they all come down for some scran, then we'll go over and mingle. Keep it casual men, we don't want too many questions. After that we'll head up to bed nice and early and aim to be first on the coach tomorrow morning with nobody the wiser. Then Bob's your uncle, we'll be on our way to Pompey.'

'What if they realize we're not part of the coach party?' Jimmy asked anxiously.

'This bunch wouldn't notice if their arses were on fire,' the Admiral snorted dismissively, 'Have you had a shufti Jimmy lad? There can't be anybody in that bunch under eighty five. Now come on, I need a drink.'

For about half an hour they sat in the bar in companionable silence. Even Jimmy seemed to lighten up a bit, right up to the point when he said suddenly, 'But what about Pickles Sir? How are we going to sneak him onto the coach? They're bound to notice that there wasn't a bloody dog on board before they got here.' The Admiral opened his mouth to answer, then closed it again when one wasn't immediately forthcoming. Bugger, this was going to take some working out. He sighed. Sometimes he wished that others would assume the mantle of leader every now and again. Being consistently looked up to as the man with all the answers could be very trying sometimes. But then this was why he was the only one of the three of them who made it to Admiral.

He smiled back at his friends with condescending benevolence. 'Well Jimmy boy, as a wise man once said, *If you can't dazzle 'em with brilliance, baffle 'em with bullshit.* It's always worked for me...'

They lapsed back into silence while the Admiral wracked his brains to come up with the slight adjustment to the plan to accommodate a large Springer spaniel. Nothing sprang to mind however, and he was actually quite relieved when the geriatric rabble rousers began trickling in for dinner, forcing him to put an end to his imaginings. Without regret, he decided that it was a problem for tomorrow. He didn't know how, but he'd get old Pickles on that coach hook or by crook.

Chapter Eleven

I t's just after seven thirty when we get on the road. Did I mention little Isaac is an early riser?

Still we should beat the traffic at Exeter, but then of course we'll run into it at Bristol, not to mention Birmingham and Manchester – oh the joys of motorway travelling. Tory's BMW accommodates all of us easily, even with the car seat, although I think it might be a tad cosy when Noah joins us in Glasgow.

'We'll drive for about four hours, or until Isaac wakes up, and then we'll stop and grab something to eat. How does that sound to everybody?' There's a general murmuring of agreement from everyone but Dotty and Isaac who are both sound asleep.

Obviously I'm Tory's co-driver and will take over when she gets tired. Both Mabel and Emily offered their services, but we managed to turn them down without being too offensive. So there we go, our plan, such as it is, is sorted. It's time to get this show on the road.

By the time we reach Bristol Isaac is screaming and Dotty is bouncing up and down indicating her need for the toilet. 'Didn't you take her out for a wee before we left?' I shout over the din in the back.

'I tried, but you know what Dotty's like in the mornings, it's all I could do to get her to leave the bed. It was only when she heard me start the car that she deigned to get up. CAN YOU STICK HIS DUMMY IN MABEL?'

'How far away is the next service station?' I ask, wondering whether I should start searching for tissues, or borrow one of

Isaac's nappies.

'Michael Woods is only five miles. It's not as far north as I'd hoped, but I don't think Isaac's going to last much longer.'

'Ditto Dotty,' I say, trying to put the little dog down on the floor – reasoning that Tory's posh upholstery is a better place to do her business than my only pair of clean jeans.

A few minutes later we're pulling into the service station and we all breathe a sigh of relief as Tory finally stops the car. I quickly put on Dotty's leash and take her to the nearest patch of grass. I can almost hear her relief as she squats down. I know how she feels...

I get back to the car as the discussion about what to eat seems to be getting a little heated. Tory is still in the driver's seat feeding Isaac and she shrugs her shoulders as the two matrons in the back debate which exciting motorway fare they should opt for - a KFC or a Burger King...

'Blimey,' I murmur, getting into the passenger seat, 'It's only ten thirty, a bit early for fast food if you ask me.'

'So you don't want a Whopper then?' she asks drily with a grin.

'Can't you just go to both?' I ask when there's a slight break in the arguing. There's a short silence as though the thought hadn't occurred to either of them. I sigh, 'Come on then ladies, I'll go with you. Do you want KFC or Burger King Tory?'

'Mmm, think I'll go for a bacon and cheese fillet burger courtesy of Colonel Sanders,' she responds licking her lips, 'And a decaf coffee.'

'Healthy,' I say climbing out of the car and shutting the door.

'I have to share it with Dotty,' she calls after me self righteously. I laugh and flip her the finger, then hurry to catch the two old dears who, judging by the speed they're going, are either famished or having the same problem as Dotty.

The inside of the service station is heaving. We all take care of business then meet back at the entrance. Looking up at the signs, I groan. KFC is on the other side of the motorway which means we'll need to go over the footbridge. Taking charge I turn to my companions.

'Emily, you get into the Burger King queue here and grab a Whopper for me and whatever you want, while I go to KFC over the other side with Mabel. We'll see you back at the car.' Before they have chance to protest, I take Mabel's arm and steer her towards the entrance to the motorway footbridge. As we push open the door to the stairs I can just hear Emily's, 'What did you say you wanted dear...?'

~*~

'I can't believe we're stopping already. These geriatrics have got bladders the size of bollocking hamsters. We'll never get to Pompey at this rate'

'Well I have to say I wouldn't mind using the facilities if we're stopping Sir.' The Admiral glared at Jimmy, then sighed. 'I suppose it might be a good opportunity to give Pickles a wee while we're at it,' he conceded, bending down to the spaniel snoozing at his feet.

'And we can grab some scran if we're getting off Charlie, I'm bloody starving.'

All in all, *Operation Leg Over* did seem to be back on course. After some successful mingling last night, they'd got up nice and early as the Admiral had reluctantly decided that sacrificing breakfast was the only way to make sure they were first on the coach.

Consequently they were now cosily ensconced on the back row with Pickles under the seat. It had all been very easy really. Nobody seemed to have the least idea that they were newcomers to the party – either that, or they weren't bothered. Most of the old boys seemed intent on getting blathered in honour of their sea going days, and looking at the resulting casualties this morning, the Admiral privately wondered whether some of them would actually survive the trip.

There was only one other old fellow sharing the back seat with them, who seemed disinclined to talk. After bidding them good morning, he'd nodded off and been asleep ever since.

They decided to wait until everyone got off the coach before making their own move. That way, no one would cotton on to their additional four legged passenger. However, when their back seat companion still didn't move a full five minutes after everyone else had left, Hugo spoke up in a loud whisper, 'We're not going to have time to get anything to eat if we dinna go in a minute Charlie. Everyone will start coming back and then Pickles'll be spotted.'

'Give him a nudge and ask him if he wants us to fetch him anything,' the Admiral instructed Jimmy who was sitting closest. The small man coughed and leaned towards the recumbent gentleman. 'Sir, would you like us to bring you anything?' The man was silent. Jimmy glanced back at the other two with a frown before trying again.

'Sir, I said, would you like us to get you something to eat?' Still nothing.

'Give him a shove Jimmy, and for God's sake speak up man, they're nearly all bloody deaf in here.' The Admiral poked Jimmy to illustrate the action he wanted his friend to take.

'DO YOU WANT SOME SCRAN SIR?' Jimmy shouted in the man's ear before giving him a small prod. Leisurely, almost in seeming slow motion, the man's torso toppled to the side until his head came to rest on the window.

'BLOODY HELL, HE'S DEAD,' Jimmy shouted in panic. 'OH MY GOD WHAT ARE WE GOING TO DO?'

'Keep your bollocking voice down Jimmy,' the Admiral hissed, 'And don't be so ridiculous. We can't be sure the bloke's popped his clogs. He could just be in a deep sleep.

'We'll leave him here while we go and do the necessaries. By the time we get back, he'll be wide awake and we'll all be having a good laugh.'

The Admiral ushered the other two quickly down the bus after deciding to leave Pickles where he was – it would take too much time now to take him out. He wasn't worried - the Springer had the bladder of a rhinoceros and he was tucked nicely under the seat snoring.

They hurried across the tarmac and a couple of minutes later arrived at the entrance to the service station. 'Right,' the Admiral ordered, taking charge, 'Heads first, then scran.'

'Ooh, there's a KFC,' Jimmy enthused smacking his lips, 'Who's for a Bargain Bucket?'

The Admiral sighed. 'Right Jimmy, you join the queue while we do what we need to do, then we'll swap over.'

When he came back five minutes later, the Admiral fully expected Jimmy to be near the front of the line, but to his consternation, the small man hadn't moved. He was standing transfixed.

'What the bloody hell's wrong with you Jimmy?' he grumbled when he got close enough for the small man to spot him, 'You look like a lost fart in a haunted milk bottle.'

Jimmy pointed towards the counter. 'Isn't that Tory's friend Kit?' With a sudden sinking feeling, the Admiral turned his head in the direction of Jimmy's arm. 'And what's she doing with your Mabel...?'

~*~

Florence sat in the hospital waiting room and determinedly read her magazine. She was alone, having insisted that Neil stay at home to look after Pepé.

She felt strangely calm now the time had finally come, and the decision to have the cancerous lung removed had not been that difficult at the end of the day. She wasn't ready to leave Kit yet, or Neil come to that.

She smiled to herself as she admitted at long last, that her agent was the love of her life. If she came through the operation, she would make sure he knew it. He'd loved her for years, waiting patiently while she dithered over making a formal commitment, using Kit as an excuse not to move away from Dartmouth. But now it was time. Her beloved niece needed to spread her wings and Flo needed to let her go.

There was only one more thing that had to be finished before she allowed Neil to take care of her as he'd wanted to for so long, and Florence was determined she would be well enough to see it done.

~*~

'Bollocking bollocks.' The Admiral's expletive was heartfelt but fortunately not loud enough to carry. He grabbed Jimmy's arm and waved frantically at Hugo who was coming towards them.

Uncertainly the Scotsman waved back and the Admiral ground his teeth in frustration. 'Get your arse over here Scotty,' he hissed as loudly as he dared, and, sensing something wrong, Hugo quickened his pace. 'What's wrong Char...' he started, only to be yanked behind a vending machine.

Keeping one eye on the two women at the counter, the Admiral calculated the time it would take them to reach the entrance. They couldn't afford to be spotted at this late stage, but they couldn't hang around here for too long either, or they'd miss the coach – not to mention the fact that Pickles was still on it. *Operation Leg Over* had never been so precarious.

'Right men,' he whispered to the others, 'I've got a plan. See that group of women coming towards us, we're going to follow them, try and blend in.'

'Why?' the Scotsman asked in a heated whisper, 'I thought we were getting some scran.'

'If you ever want to have your night of delight with old Alice, you'll get going now Scotty. I'll fill you in later.' Taking a deep breath, the Admiral looked at each of his oppos. 'Don't move until I give the signal.

He popped his head round the vending machine as the first of the ladies passed them. 'Now,' he whispered urgently, and a couple of seconds later they were surrounded by the gaggle of women heading towards the entrance.

'Bloody hell that was close,' Jimmy breathed as they finally climbed back on the coach. 'I thought they were going to spot us for sure.'

'Did that woman give you her phone number Charlie,' asked Hugo pulling himself up behind Jimmy.

'Don't be so bloody ridiculous,' the Admiral answered, tucking the piece of paper into his trouser pocket.

They hurried down to the back of the bus, relieved that they weren't the last back. Seating themselves back down, Jimmy and Hugo fussed around with their bits and pieces, while the Admiral bent down to give the still snoring Pickles a quick stroke. Then, knowing they couldn't put it off any longer, they all looked towards the occupant in the corner. Who hadn't moved.

'Bloody hell, he IS dead,' Hugo said in awe.

'Shhh, keep your voice down Scotty.' The Admiral glanced furtively around to check if anyone had heard Hugo's diagnosis. Luckily the seats nearest the back were still awaiting their occupants.

'Hadn't we better tell the driver?'

'If we tell the driver, we'll have to stop and wait here for someone to come and take him away. Who knows how long that will take? I vote we keep schtum until we get to Pompey. Let them sort it out at Nelson.'

'We can't do that,' said Jimmy aghast.

'Why not?' the Admiral answered matter of factly. 'It's not like he's got anywhere else to go.'

'It dinna feel right Charlie, Jimmy's right about that.'

'Look at him,' the Admiral argued, pointing towards the corpse, 'He looks as happy as Larry. For all we know, making this trip might have been the most important thing in the world to him. How can we deny him one last opportunity to see the sacred home of the Royal Navy?'

'Well he's not likely to see much is he?'

'He does look happy though.'

'How can you say he looks happy? He's got his eyes closed.'

'But there's a definite smile on his face.'

'Shouldn't we find out his name?'

'Good thinking Jimmy, check his jacket pockets.'

'Why can't you check his pockets Sir?'

'Don't be so bloody squeamish. It's not like you've never seen a dead body before.'

'No, but I've never seen one on a bus.'

The Admiral sighed and was just about to swap seats with Jimmy when the four men sharing the seats in front of them boarded the coach and wobbled precariously towards to the back.

'Hold your positions,' the Admiral whispered, 'And stand at ease.'

'We're actually sitting Sir,' Jimmy whispered back helpfully, earning him The Look.

'Act casual men,' Charles Shackleford continued, speaking from the side of his mouth, 'And whatever you do, do not, I repeat, do not, draw attention to the corpse.'

The three men immediately attempted to look busy, only stopping their slightly manic actions to smile nervously as the four men eventually made it to the back and sat down.

Finally, much to their combined relief, the coach started to move, making its way slowly back towards the motorway. The Admiral turned to clap his companions on their back, murmuring, 'That's it men, we've done it, we're home free. Pompey here we come...'

'I say Tom, has the bus driver put some kind of heating on? I'm getting the most bloody uncomfortable warm damp air floating up my trouser leg from under the seat. Almost feels like I'm being licked...'

~*~

The closer we get to Bloodstone Tower, the more nervous I'm becoming. Not that I've had an awful lot of time to brood after being relegated to the back once we picked up Noah – what with keeping the peace between Mabel and Emily, and watching over Isaac.

I never realized that pensioners could be so argumentative. I mean, I know the Admiral can be a bit difficult (understatement of the year), but Mabel and Emily have been at it since Exeter. It's difficult to see how they can be such good friends – they don't seem to have a positive thing to say to each other. I can't help but wonder if Tory and I will be the same when we get into our dotage, then have to concede it's very likely given the sheer number of things we argue about already...

'How much longer have we got Noah?' I ask after listening to why Mabel can't eat baked beans for the fifth time.

'About another hour,' Noah responds grinning knowingly at me through his rear view mirror.

'I don't mind taking over for a while if you're getting tired,' I say sweetly through gritted teeth.

'I'm fine Kit, don't you worry. Relax and enjoy the ride.' He finishes the last sentence with a wink and I want to punch him.

Turning round in the front passenger seat, Tory smiles at me in sympathy. 'Why don't you try and sleep Kitty Kat, I'll wake you up in plenty of time to make yourself respectable.'

'Thanks, you're a true friend,' I mutter sarcastically.

'That reminds me Kit, I was reading about this new treatment in the newspaper, I think it's called *Wrinklesmooth*, or is it *Smoothwrinkle*? Anyway, it's supposed to do wonders for your fine lines. I've kept the article for you.' I look over at Mabel's face on the slight off chance she's being sarcastic, but all I see is an earnest desire to help.

Before I get chance to respond, Emily interrupts irritably, 'Why do you always have to take up so much room Mabel. You keep elbowing me in the ribs.'

'It's not me, it's Kit,' Mabel protests, 'She's the one taking up the space. Since she got into the back, there's not been room to swing a cat.' She turns to me. 'Have you thought about going on a diet dear? I heard that the one you have to do in Cambridge is very good. Mind you, that's if you've got the time to go to Cambridge of course.'

'Are you barking Mabel? Why would they have to go to Cambridge to do a diet?'

'I've no idea Emily, I think they have a different way of eating in Cambridge. Perhaps it helps with *the bowels*.' The last two words are a loud whisper directly in Emily's ear.

'ENOUGH,' I shout. The two of them look at me blankly and Isaac starts crying...

I'd forgotten just how magnificent the Scottish Highlands are. After making one last stop to give little Isaac a break (and me I think), we're finally approaching Loch Long. Craggy mountains tower above us in every direction, clothed in stately green and purple, and occasionally dappled sunlight as the clouds part briefly. Then the road twists and suddenly the loch appears in all its mysterious beauty. A light mist hovers over the surface creating an otherworldly eerie feeling, almost as though we've stepped back in time. Even Mabel and Emily are silent as the car speeds like a ghost towards Bloodstone Tower.

Ten minutes later, Noah's turning the car into an almost hidden driveway and Dotty suddenly sits up on Tory's knee. The last time we were here we were on the run, and only stayed for a couple of days, but the little dog clearly remembers.

As the car comes to a halt outside the Tower, I'm struck anew by just how dilapidated the building is. The thought of trying to renovate such a mausoleum fills me with trepidation.

Apprehensively I wait in the back next to Isaac while the two matrons clamber out of the car, arguing about who should use the toilet first. Dotty of course has no such issue and is busy christening every patch of grass she can sniff out. As Tory comes round the back to lift her son out of his car seat, I have no more excuses to linger, so taking a deep breath, I climb out into the early evening gloom and stretch my cramped muscles.

'Ah, guid eenin, hou's aw wi ye.'

I feel myself relaxing slightly as I hear the lilting tones of Aileen, the resident housekeeper, come cook, come... well, pretty much everything at Bloodstone Tower. She's wiping her hands on her apron as she makes her way along an uneven path that leads from the kitchen round the back. I feel my mouth water as I recall her amazing baking skills.

Dotty obviously remembers too and wastes no time in dashing towards the plump woman in a flurry of barking and wagging tail. Laughing, Aileen bends down to fuss the little dog, then straightens up to include us all in a wide smile. 'Walcome tae Bloodstone, it's been donkies since a last saw ye.

'Noo whaur's that wee bairn.' Tory walks forward with a smile of her own, always happy to show off her son. Aileen puts out her hand and gently strokes the little boy's hair. 'Och ma sweet wean, he's a bonny lad and nae mistake,' she breathes, 'And Hou's aw wi ye and that braw man o yours?'

I watch, happy to stay in the background as Noah strolls up to his wife and leans down to give Aileen a kiss, causing the elderly woman to go the colour of a tomato. 'Aw, gaun yersel,' she splutters waving her apron at him.

Then suddenly my heart begins thumping erratically as Jason comes round the corner accompanied by a small woman with flaming red hair. 'Could this be the proverbial 'bit on the side?' I wonder, feeling a sharp pang of jealousy.

Awkwardly, wondering what the hell's wrong with me, I hang back slightly, watching as Jason, in complete contrast to our visit last year, welcomes his visitors with warmth and enthusiasm. Smiling he introduces the woman next to him as Nicole -apparently she's Aileen's niece from London – and then returns the favour.

'Come in, come in.' Aileen draws everyone towards the kitchen and after a couple of moments, there's only me and Jason left. I look down at the floor and scuff my trainer in the dirt like a five year old.

'Hi,' Jason murmurs softly. I look up and my heart slams against my ribs at the raw desire in his face. He reaches out slowly and strokes my cheek, then his hand slides round to the back of my head and he draws me towards him, his eyes never leaving mine. Finally our lips touch and his kiss is soft and searching, in complete contrast to the hunger in his eyes. Helplessly I reach up to pull him to me and his mouth slants across mine, deepening the kiss.

It feels like I'm coming home, and it scares the crap out of me.

Chapter Twelve

T his is the third bloody stop and our ship mate hasn't moved a muscle. Surely somebody's got to notice soon.'

'I don't think this lot would notice if you stuck a bloody grenade underneath 'em.' The Admiral shook his head. 'And to think these sorry excuses were once supposedly our finest naval officers. Makes a body think. It's a good job the RN had the likes of me to steer 'em in the right direction.'

He was totally oblivious to Hugo and Jimmy's incredulous glances at each other as he watched the occupants of the coach totter across the car park. Sighing, he looked down at his watch. By his reckoning they should arrive at Nelson just in time for Scotty to have a quick spruce up before his rendezvous with Alice. Once they'd delivered the Scotsman to HMS Nelson, the Admiral's job would be done until the next morning. Then all he had to do was get his charge back up to Bloodstone Tower none the worse for wear, which should be a piece of cake providing old Scotty didn't over exert himself in the meantime of course. When he'd finished congratulating himself on a brilliantly executed plan, he glanced over at their silent companion. He hoped the coach driver would notice him before he parked up to let the cleaners in.

'We've got another slight problem, Charlie,' Hugo interrupted the Admiral's smug contemplation with an embarrassed cough.

The Admiral turned to him and frowned. 'What kind o' problem?'

'The thing is.... what ah mean is .....'

'Spit it out Scotty' the Admiral interrupted irritably, 'You're acting like a bloody fart in a trance.'

Visibly gathering himself together, Hugo took a deep breath, 'The thing is,' he finished in a rush, 'Ah dinna have any smalls.'

The Admiral stared at him for a second thinking how often pride comes before a fall. How he could have made such a small but epic mistake? It wasn't like he could lend Hugo any of his own underpants. He was down to turning his underwear inside out after all, and old Scotty was supposed to be tarting himself up for an assignation.

All this bloody way and the whole thing could go tits up on account of no clean underwear.

'Right.' The Admiral took charge and turned to Jimmy. 'Go with Scotty and sort him out a pair of clean undies. He'll need socks too. No woman likes to wake up beside a man wearing sweaty socks.' The Admiral was completely oblivious to the fact that most women don't like to wake up next to a man wearing socks at all...

'I'll keep an eye on the coach driver and I won't let the bus leave without you.' He eyed each of them with narrowed eyes. 'This could make or break *Operation Leg Over*, so don't get it wrong men. You have fifteen minutes.

The Admiral sighed as he watched his two oppos scurry towards the services. This was a shot across the bow and no mistake. He'd forgotten just how easily a plan can fall apart when no attention is paid to the little things. He glanced over at his silent companion and wondered if he should give him a book...

Ten minutes later the Admiral was not ashamed to admit he was becoming slightly alarmed as he watched the coach driver through the window trying to round up his elderly charges. Nearly everyone was back on the bus, but there was no sign of Scotty and Jimmy. He was just wondering if a repeat performance of his famous faint at Greenwich would be called for, when he saw them hurrying across the car park. They climbed on board, just as the driver returned to the coach looking, the Admiral thought, a trifle frazzled.

'Is everybody back on the bus?' the driver yelled. Unfortunately nobody appeared to be taking a blind bit of notice. He tried again. 'Is there anybody still in the toilet?' When he still had no response, he shook his head and shrugged his shoulders. A couple of minutes later they were on the road again.

As the coach swung back onto the motorway, both Jimmy and Hugo looked a bit worse for wear. The Admiral privately wondered if old Scotty would be able to do the deed after all the exercise he'd had. Still, as long he'd managed to pick a pair of clean drawers and socks, the option was still open to him.

'There wasn't that much choice to be honest Sir,' Jimmy wheezed, 'But we did the best we could.' Hugo held up a pair of black socks, perfect apart from a pair of puckered lips and the words *kiss me* embroidered on the side.

'Tacky,' muttered the Admiral, 'But I suppose beggars can't be choosers. What about underpants? I dread to think what bloody slogan they've got written on 'em.'

Jimmy handed over a remarkably small package for the Admiral's inspection. Frowning, Charles Shackleford ripped open the packet and watched disbelievingly as a minute pair of briefs landed on his lap.

'What the bloody hell do you call these?' he asked holding up the underwear which in his opinion was unlikely to cover little Isaac's tackle, let alone Scotty's.

'They're called budgie smugglers,' offered Hugo smugly, pointing to the picture of a parrot on the packet. 'I think Alice might want seconds after she cops sight of me in these...'

It was nearly five o'clock before their coach finally turned into HMS Nelson, and it took another twenty minutes for its occupants to totter off. Well, all but one anyway. Jimmy was getting very anxious as it became obvious that no one was actually going to notice that one of their number was in fact dead.

'What are we going to say to the driver?' Jimmy hissed to the Admiral as they watched the last of the group get off. 'I mean, they might think we bumped him off.'

'We're not going to say anything Jimmy boy. The driver'll soon spot him when he does his recce. At least the old boy made it to Nelson, and I'm sure he's looking down from paradise a very happy sailor right this minute.'

'I just hope it does nae give the bus driver the fright of his bloody life,' Hugo muttered as they started down the centre aisle. Pulling Pickles out from under the seat, the Admiral gave a last glance at their recently departed ship mate and nodded respectfully. Then he clambered out of the back seats and hurriedly made his way after Jimmy and Hugo.

~*~

'So where do you think that sorry husband of mine and his interfering old windbag of a so called friend have taken your father?'

Jason shrugs his shoulders at Emily's scathing question, and with an apologetic glance towards Tory, answers, 'Who knows what, where or why regarding Charles Shackleford.'

'Don't worry about offending me Jason,' Tory responds to his remorseful look, 'I've long since developed a thick skin where my father's concerned. His actions frequently baffle me every bit as much as everyone else.'

We're sitting in front of a roaring fire in the Great Hall. Although it's technically summer in Scotland, the evening temperature couldn't be described as balmy, especially considering all the fresh air coming through the ill fitting windows in Bloodstone Tower.

Aileen is busy preparing supper, but fearing we all might starve to death in the meantime, she's left us a large batch of her amazing shortbread and enough tea to supply an army. Dotty of course is guarding the shortbread...

Tory helps herself to tea and a large slice of shortbread, having just returned from putting Isaac to bed. Biting into the buttery sweetness, she closes her eyes in bliss and leans back against

Noah who pulls her close to him to plant a quick kiss on the top of her head.

As I watch them, I can't help but wonder if Jason and I will ever get to that level of easy affection, and then question whether I've actually got it in me to be that close to anyone.

I look over at the object of my thoughts to find him staring at me intently. Our eyes meet briefly, then he turns away to listen to Mabel. I can feel him treating me with kid gloves – as if he fears I might bolt if he applies any pressure. And he could be right. Sighing, I tune back into the conversation.

'I'm certain Charles and Jimmy will look after Hugo, Jason,' Mabel is saying contritely. 'I know my husband's very fond of your father and I'm sure he wouldn't do anything stupid.' We all look at her silently.

'Well there's nothing we can do until we hear from them,' Jason responds matter of factly when nobody ventures to speak. 'And I'm sure you're right Mabel, they're grown men after all. They're probably holed up in some hotel room as we speak, watching the TV and arguing over what to order for room service.' The resulting nodding of heads is enthusiastic if slightly doubtful...

'But if I don't hear anything by tomorrow evening,' he continues, 'I think it will be time to call the police.'

Both Aileen and her niece join us for supper and despite everyone's concerns, the meal is a light hearted affair, mostly due to Jason and Noah doing their best to keep spirits high. I can't help but notice how relaxed Nicole seems, joking and laughing as though she's been here forever. She blushed a little at first every time Noah engaged her in conversation, but that soon stopped and now she seems completely comfortable in the presence of Hollywood royalty.

'What made you decide to come up to the wilds of Scotland Nicole?' Tory asks curiously, obviously dying to know if it's a broken heart she's running away from.

'I just needed a break from the hustle and bustle of London,' the petite redhead answers cautiously. 'My grandmother arrived unexpectedly over from France to stay with my mum. They have a very...er...volatile relationship, and sometimes they can get a little too much, so I decided to take myself off and come stay with Aunt Aileen.'

'Aye, it's true, they're French,' Aileen throws in, as if that answers everything.

'So how long are you stopping?' I try so hard to keep my question casual and non aggressive and I must have succeeded because no one is looking at me like I'm a budding axe murderer.

'I...I'm not sure,' Nicole responds, glancing at Jason, which of course makes me want to go out and sharpen a hatchet somewhere...

'Nicole's offered to stay for a while and look after my father,' Jason interrupts, smiling down at her.' Scratch that, I think I'll go for a machete.

'Bit of a life saver really,' Jason continues, completely oblivious to my homicidal imaginings, 'Or it would have been had the Admiral not decided to take matters into his own hands.' For the first time in my entire life, I want to put my arms around Tory's father and give him a big hug...

'That's so kind,' smiles Tory, her voice so saccharine sweet that I look at her in amazement.

'Well hopefully the Laird will be back before long.' Nicole gives an equally warm smile back, 'But until then, I'm trying to make myself useful.'

'I'm sure you are,' I mutter under my breath.

'That was a beautiful meal Aileen,' Tory declares warmly, with a side glance at my sour face, 'It was just what the doctor ordered after being on the road all day. I hope you'll excuse me, but I need to take Dotty out for a quick walk before bed. You fancy joining me Kit?'

'What about me?' asks Noah plaintively, 'Don't I deserve a romantic walk by the loch with my beautiful wife?'

'One of us needs to be here for Isaac sweetheart,' Tory responds, standing up, 'And anyway, I thought you and Jason could give Aileen a hand with the dishes.' The last is said with a mischievous grin as she pulls me up from the table. 'Come on Kitty Kat, go grab your jacket.'

Five minutes later we're dragging a reluctant Dotty from her place by the fire (or more significantly, the shortbread) through the main doors and down towards the loch.

The night is actually surprisingly warm, and more importantly, the horrible tiny black midges that are so rife this time of year have retired to bed. Walking slowly along the lochside footpath, we watch Dotty regain her enthusiasm for outdoors as she gallops backwards and forwards in and out of the heather bordering the trail on the other side.

'So what was that all about?' I ask, watching the little dog pause for a breather. 'That's sooo niiiice of you,' I mimic spitefully as she looks over at me with her eyebrows raised.

'Have you never heard of the phrase, *keep your friends close, but your enemies closer*?'

'What are you talking about?' I respond irritably, stopping to throw a pebble into the inky black water.

'You were doing everything but launching yourself over the table to scratch her eyes out Kit. That's so not like you. I just wanted to take you out before you said anything you might regret.'

I opened my mouth to argue, then slump, muttering, 'I didn't think anyone noticed.'

'Don't worry I'm sure they didn't, but they don't know you like I do. I thought a walk might calm you down a bit.'

'You don't think that Jason... that what your father said has any truth in it do you?' I ask hesitantly, hating the anxiety in my voice. Tory snorts inelegantly, 'Since when did you ever believe anything my old man comes out with? You know what he's like Kit, he opens his mouth before he engages his brain most of the time.'

'So you don't think she's attracted to Jason?'

'I didn't say that. If she's heterosexual, she's attracted. After all, even I can appreciate that Captain Buchannan's pretty damn scrumptious when he's not scowling.'

I groan, stopping so abruptly that Dotty crashes into my ankles. 'What do you think I should do?'

'I think you need to decide what it is that you want Kit. I think Jason loves you, but as long as you keep dithering, you're leaving the playground free for other people to come and join in. And he won't wait forever. You know that.'

'It's not just Jason,' I cry out in frustration, 'It's all this.' I wave my arms around encompassing the craggy terrain and the distant shadowed stones of Bloodstone Tower. 'Why can't he just be happy to settle in Dartmouth?'

'You knew how much he loved his home when you first started dating,' Tory responds quietly. 'Did you think he'd never come back?'

'I don't know what I thought. It's all come so suddenly. Why in hell did Noah have to agree to help fund such a bloody mad project?'

To my surprise Tory laughs. 'It's just the kind of thing Noah loves to get involved in. It wouldn't surprise me if he wants to do some of the work himself. Come on Kit, where's your sense of adventure? Just imagine this place when it's been renovated, it's going to be fabulous. Can't you see yourself as lady of the manor?'

'I think that honour belongs to Jason's grandmother, and by the sound of things she's likely to outlive us all.' Against my will, I start to chuckle. 'Can you just picture your father standing in his underpants at the bathroom door?'

'I'd rather not,' Tory giggles, linking her arm in mine as we finally turn back. 'And what about the time she thought you were the ghost of the Lady of the Tower come to take her away.'

'Not to mention you tripping over the chamber pot in her bedroom.'

We're both laughing helplessly by now. 'Oh my God,' I splutter finally, no wonder she doesn't welcome us with open arms.'

'Have you seen her since we got here?' Tory asks when we finally subside. I shake my head in the gloom. 'I don't think she's ventured out of her room. I think Aileen takes her meals up on a tray. Or maybe Nicole does it now she's making herself useful.

'She'll probably adore someone so tiny and dainty,' I continue ruefully, 'And of course there's all that gorgeous red hair, there's got to be some Scottish in there somewhere.'

'Maybe she's got a fiery temper to go with it,' Tory retorts before turning round to shout Dotty, 'A lot of women are not as biddable as me and you.' I look at her disbelievingly, just in time to see her grin.

'I can think of a lot of ways to describe you honey, but biddable? Never.' Noah's voice echoes out of the shadows and a couple of seconds later he looms out of the darkness.

'Where did you come from?' Tory asks laughing softly as he leans down to kiss her.

'Dishes are all washed, so I came to tell you ladies that there's coffee and digestives awaiting you in the hall.'

'Have you eaten all the shortbread?'

'I wouldn't dare...'

Jason is sitting alone by the fire in the Great Hall, and Dotty wastes no time in dashing to climb onto his knee. I swear she actually looked back at me with a smirk as she made herself comfortable. 'Have Mabel and Emily gone to bed?' I ask softly, collapsing next to him with a sigh. He nods his head and leans back to put his arm around me. 'Did you enjoy your stroll?'

'It was beautiful as always,' Tory enthuses, sitting on the sofa opposite, 'I just love the peace and quiet up here, the sense of timelessness.'

'Well that's good honey because we'll be seeing a lot more of it,' Noah smiles sinking down next to her.

'How are the plans for Chez Bloodstone coming along?' I ask, making no attempt to keep the slight sarcasm out of my voice.

Jason glances over at me but refrains from making a comment about my mockery, which of course makes me feel like a petulant child. When he finally speaks, his tone is mild, giving nothing away. 'I'm hoping we'll be a position to start the work early in the

New Year. Noah reckons he'll be between movies in the spring, and I think he fancies a bit of hard labour.'

'Yeah, well, if I'm gonna stand any chance of landing a TV advert for Pepsi, I need to start getting some practice in,' Noah quips. The two men grin at each other in perfect accord and it suddenly occurs to me that they genuinely like one another.

'Mmm, coffee, Cointreau and home-made shortbread,' mumbles Tory with her mouth full, 'If ever there was a ménage à trois made in heaven.'

Relieved at the change of subject, I lean forward to grab a piece of shortbread.

'Is your grandmother okay?' I ask Jason, 'I haven't seen her since we got here.'

'And I don't think you're likely to,' Jason responds drily, twirling his glass of Old Pulteney single malt, 'You know what she's like when we have guests in the house.'

'What does she think of your plans to renovate Bloodstone Tower?' Tory asks curiously. Jason grimaces and takes a large swallow of his whisky. 'I haven't told her yet. Or my father.'

'Will he try and stop you from going ahead?' Tory questions with concern.

'He hasn't really got a choice,' Jason answers ruefully, 'The alternatives are to try and sell, or let the whole thing fall into wrack and ruin. And as you can see, we're already well on the way to the second option.'

A sudden cry on the baby monitor puts an end to the conversation. Tory pops the last piece of shortbread into her mouth and gets to her feet. 'That's our cue,' she laughs, picking up the still snoring Dotty, 'Bedtime, though somehow I think Dotspot will be the only one doing much sleeping.'

'Tell me about it,' sighs Noah getting up and following his wife to the stairs, 'Now if only we were staying awake to indulge in wild passionate sex...'

The door shuts behind them and we sit in silence for a few minutes. 'Do you think your father will accept the change easily?' I ask softly eventually.

'I have no idea,' Jason responds tiredly, 'I was waiting until he felt better before breaking the news.'

There's a pause as he turns towards me. 'I have no choice about this Kit,' he says softly, earnestly, 'I hope you understand that. If I don't do something, we will almost certainly lose Bloodstone Tower, and whatever my father thinks of my plans to save it, the alternative really will break his heart.'

I nod slowly, knowing in my heart that we've reached crunch time. If I refuse to back him in this, our relationship will be over. I lean forward and cup his face gently. 'Let's go to bed,' I murmur and lean forward to kiss him lightly. I just have time to see the momentary anxiety in his eyes, then, with a sigh, he pulls me across his lap and we both stop thinking completely.

Chapter Thirteen

It was just after midnight and both the Admiral and Jimmy were having trouble sleeping. After dropping Hugo off to prepare for his night of potential debauchery, they'd managed to get a bed for the night in a small guesthouse not far from Nelson. It was in a less than salubrious area, but it was the only one that would take dogs at such short notice.

The fish and chips they'd consumed earlier were unfortunately lying like a lump of lead in the Admiral's stomach, playing havoc with his ulcer.

But the main reason they were both tossing and turning was the racket coming from directly below their room.

'Are they having a bollocking party or what?' the Admiral finally grumbled, sitting up, 'They sound like herd of bloody elephants. There's no way either of us is going to get any shut eye with that cake and arse party going on.' He sighed and pushed back the covers. 'Come on Jimmy, we'll just have to go and tell 'em to pipe down.'

'But I haven't brought a dressing gown Sir,' protested Jimmy as the Admiral strode towards the door.

'Don't be such a bloody nancy,' retorted the Admiral, carefully peeking out on to the landing, 'You've got more clothes on than if you were attending divisions.' Jimmy glanced down at the brushed cotton pyjamas covering his vest and long johns. 'Anybody would think it was bloody February the way you're buttoned up.'

'I feel the cold,' Jimmy protested, wincing as his bare feet hit the floor. 'Hang on a minute Sir, I need to put my socks on.'

The Admiral sighed and waited impatiently as the small man rummaged around his bag for a pair of socks. 'Right, I'm ready Sir, let's sort these ruffians out.'

The Admiral frowned at his friend's sudden enthusiasm. 'Have you been drinking out o' that hip flask again Jimmy?'

Jimmy shook his head. 'It's just that sometimes I forget I was a Master At Arms. Keeping the peace was my job for nearly thirty years, and the fact is Admiral, once a Master At Arms, always a Master At Arms. It never really leaves you Sir, and if we get into a spot of bother, I can still remember my martial arts training.'

The Admiral stared nonplussed as Jimmy bent his front knee and pushed his back leg out behind him, then punched out with his arms before bringing them down in a chopping motion.

'See,' he panted, dropping his arms and straightening up with a wince, before finally executing a small bow. The Admiral simply shook his head, ordered Pickles to stay, and beckoned the small man out into the hall.

They tiptoed along the landing and stuck their heads over the banister to look down the stairs. The noise appeared to be coming from a room across the foyer. As they listened, there was a loud cheer followed by an even louder thump.

'We'd better get in there fast Sir, before they completely trash the place.' Without waiting for the Admiral's nod, Jimmy began to creep slowly down the stairs to preserve their element of surprise. Or at least that was his intent. He actually arrived at the bottom considerably quicker as his socks turned the staircase into a makeshift ski slope. As the last three steps turned a sharp right, Jimmy missed them entirely and did an impromptu somersault over the rail, landing with a crash on top of the telephone table.

So much for surprising their quarry. 'What the bloody hell do you think you're doing Jimmy?' the Admiral hissed, hurrying down to see if his friend had done any damage to the furniture, especially given the fact that they'd probably have to pay for it.

He was just helping Jimmy up, when the door across the hall

opened, spilling out four men who looked like they ate gum shields for breakfast.

'Wot the bloody 'ell's goin on?' demanded the first one who was obviously their leader. He had an impressive comb over which in other circumstances the Admiral might have admired.

Jimmy, possibly still in shock over his spontaneous forward roll, stepped forward and said forcefully, 'Keep the damn noise down would you?' The Admiral looked over at him incredulously, then nervously back at Captain Comb-Over who was now glaring at them.

'Wot did you say?'

'Nothing, he said nothing,' the Admiral ventured in what he hoped was a suitably placatory tone.

'Didn't sound like nuffin to me,' came the all too predictable response. In three strides he was across the room and looming over them both. The Admiral took a step backwards, pulling Jimmy with him.

'I'll have you know I've had martial arts training,' Jimmy continued a little less loudly now.

Captain Comb-Over glared at him and lifted his fist. 'And I've 'ad trainin wi' this, you little tosser,' he bellowed.

With a pathetic squeak Jimmy finally saw sense and dropped to the floor, curling himself into a ball. The Admiral took a deep breath, looked down at his quivering friend, then back up at the red faced thug in front of him. Charles Shackleford was many things, but a coward wasn't one of them. However, he recognized the necessity for a strategic withdrawal when he saw it.

Keeping one eye on Captain Comb-Over, who was still standing over them, fists clenched, the Admiral bent down slowly and grabbed hold of the back of the long johns he could see poking out of Jimmy's pyjamas. Then he pulled his friend to his feet, yelled RUN at the top of his voice and made for the stairs in a sprint that would have impressed the scrum half of the England rugby team.

Three minutes later they were leaning, gasping against their bedroom door. 'So what ancient fighting technique did you call that?' the Admiral asked Jimmy, when they'd both finally got their breath back, 'The Way of the bloody Hedgehog?'

~*~

The sun is shining through the narrow windows, creating elongated beams of light when I wake. I know it's early because the sun is still low enough to penetrate the thin gaps that pass for windows in Jason's room. I glance over at the empty pillow next to me. Jason told me last night he intended to go for an early morning run. I'd actually contemplated joining him – for all of about three seconds.

I think I had quite enough exercise last night thank you very much. Remembering brings a blush to my cheeks, and unable to help myself, I stretch like a contented cat. If I had the ability, I'm sure I'd be purring now.

I made another decision last night too. As I lay in the dark listening to Jason's steady breathing, I finally realized that I never wanted to be without him. Ever. And if that means sharing his dream for Bloodstone Tower, then so be it.

I glance around the dim room trying to imagine it after a five star make over. To my surprise, I begin to see it, along with a small but burgeoning excitement. Maybe my talents do extend beyond adapting chocolate penises.

Smiling, I turn over, deciding to wait for Jason to come back before getting up. Hopefully today we'll hear from the three stooges, otherwise Freddy will definitely be running the upcoming Monster Mash tomorrow. Maybe I'd better give him a quick call. I know how he hates to be out of the loop with anything.

Climbing out of bed, I hunt around for my mobile phone, wondering if there'll be any signal in this room. We're pretty high up, so I'm hopeful – that's if I can find the bloody thing. Frowning I stand still and try to think where I put it last night. There's a pile of clothes on the old blanket box at the foot of the bed, still lying where they'd been slung last night. Maybe my phone is somewhere in there.

Padding round to the end of the bed, I pick up my jeans and t-shirt, feeling around in the pockets. Nothing. Next I hold up Jason's jeans. I can't remember giving my phone to him so there's no point in checking his pockets. I'm just about to lay them on the bed, when I notice what looks like a letter sticking out of the back pocket. Wondering if he's forgotten about it, I pull it out and stare at the envelope. I'd know that writing anywhere. It's from my Aunt Flo.

~*~

Needless to say, the noise did not abate as a result of their interference; in fact the Admiral had to concede by two am that it was considerably worse. Consequently both he and Jimmy were the exact opposite of bright eyed and bushy tailed the next morning.

The Admiral had no idea what time Hugo was likely to surface and had to admit that *Operation Leg Over* was distinctly sketchy on their withdrawal details.

'You up for breakfast Jimmy lad?' the Admiral asked when they were finally up, dressed and sitting on the bed. 'I could murder a cuppa.'

The small man nodded wearily and they made their way cautiously down the stairs. The Admiral couldn't help but notice that the telephone table was now propped up with the telephone directory, and he groaned inwardly, wondering how much it was going to cost them.

They managed to find their way to the dining room which was down another flight of stairs in what had obviously been the cellar.

'Need bloody danger money coming down these damn stairs,' muttered the Admiral, only narrowly missing giving himself an impromptu frontal lobotomy on a large beam sticking out from the wall. Ducking, he finally got past it and entered the dim room.

'Bugger,' he mumbled, stopping.

'What's wrong Sir,' asked Jimmy bumping into him from behind. Peering round the Admiral's large frame, he saw why they'd stopped. Tucking into large fry ups were their four protagonists from the night before.

Before they could scarper, a voice from their left announced cheerily, 'Good morning gents, take a seat and I'll be with you in a moment.' The voice belonged to a well-built buxom woman, wearing a large apron with her hair done à la Coronation Street's Ena Sharples.

'I feel like I've stepped into a bloody time warp,' the Admiral mumbled as they took their seats at a small table as far away from their tormentors as possible.

'Now then, what can I get you gents?' The woman was back with a pad and pencil. 'We've got tea or coffee and a full English.'

'That'll be fine, won't it Jimmy?' the Admiral was anxious not to stay any longer than they had to.

'With tea please,' Jimmy added with a nervous look towards the other tables. He couldn't believe these four louts were sitting there, bold as brass after all the fracas they caused last night, he'd a good mind to report the buggers.

'I see you had a little falling-out with my son and his friends last night,' the landlady went on to say gaily, waving at the four thugs.

'Mornin,' muttered Captain Comb-Over through a mouth full of fried bread.

'But there we go, boys will be boys,' she continued smiling fondly at her son who must have been at least forty. 'They don't mean anything by it, it's just high spirits. You know what it's like I'm sure gentlemen.' Then she bustled off into the kitchen leaving the Admiral and Jimmy to stare at each other in silence.

Half an hour later they were back in their room, and as a result of bolting down his breakfast at record speed, the Admiral now had indigestion.

'It's no good Jimmy lad,' the Admiral puffed and panted, sitting down on the bed, 'I've got to give up this gallivanting around the country. It's not doing me any good. It's time I started putting myself first.' Then, before Jimmy had chance to respond, Charles Shackleford keeled over and slid slowly to the floor.

~*~

I sit staring at the letter, an awful premonition of disaster swamping me. Why has my aunt sent something to Jason? And just as significantly, why hasn't he told me about it?

Of course it could be that there's nothing important to tell, but my heart, hammering like a sledgehammer, is telling me a different story. I turn the envelope around in my hand, then hold it up to the light to see if there's any clue as to what's written inside. There's nothing.

Placing the envelope on the bed beside me, I nibble uncertainly at my fingernails. I know I should really wait until Jason returns so I can ask him what's inside it, but equally, I know I can't. I look down again at my aunt's spider like writing and make the decision.

Heart thumping, I slide a folded A4 piece of paper out. I can see immediately that it's a letter, and my anxiety ramps up. Clumsily I unfold it, then smooth out the creases, stalling for time. I feel almost like some kind of thief.

Then, unable to help myself any longer, I look down and read.

Dear Jason

Of course you are wondering why I'm writing to you, but let me assure you that my decision to do so is purely out of concern for my niece. I know in my heart that you share my deep love for Kit, and the purpose of this letter is to reassure myself that you will do your utmost to take care of her should I die.

Although death comes to all of us eventually, I have had to face up the fact that I may well be facing the grim reaper a little earlier than I had hoped!

I have been diagnosed with cancer in my right lung and have made the decision to allow the doctors to remove it. I am going up to Lon-

don in just over a week and will stay with Neil until I'm admitted into hospital. Once the operation is performed, Neil will keep you informed as to my progress.

You are no doubt asking why I haven't told Kit about my illness. My reasons for doing so are my own, save to say that I don't want her to have to carry this burden with me.

Of course I'm hopeful of making a full recovery, and should the operation be a success, Kit does not need to know anything about it. However, should the worst happen Jason, I entreat you to take care of her.

With warmest regards

Florence Davies

I feel as though the bottom has dropped out of my world. My Aunt Flo has cancer. I think back to the times she's seemed weary, or looked pale, and I curse myself for not realizing that it wasn't just down to her age.

How could she keep something so vital from me? And why did she think it was okay to tell my boyfriend?

Her conviction that Jason loves me is a massive bloody assumption - and so is her belief that I actually *need* taking care of.

And what about Jason? The letter was written over a week ago? Was he ever going to tell me?

If he's capable of keeping something like this from me, what else is he capable of doing? Do I even know him at all? How can I ever trust him? The questions are going round and round in my head until I feel as though I'm going mad.

I think back to last night's decision to put my heart in Jason's hands. How bloody naïve can you get? I wonder if he's written back to my aunt. Perhaps the two of them have had a high old time deciding what's best for me and how I should live my life...

I'm still sitting on the bed when Jason comes into the room. Glancing at Aunt Flo's letter in my hand, he swears softly and strides over to the bed, seating himself next to me. I can smell the clean sweat from his run, the scent that is uniquely Jason and I want to burrow my head into his shoulder and stay there forever. Instead, I stare down at the contents of the letter and whisper, 'Why?'

Jason tries to put his arms around me, but stops when he feels me stiffen. I hear him sigh, no doubt trying to find the right words. Suddenly angry, I turn towards him and brandish the letter. 'Why didn't she tell me she had cancer? Why would she go into hospital to have an operation she might not survive without telling me?'

'You know why.' Jason's voice is low and filled with compassion. I want to hit him.

'She told you though,' I shout, 'So why didn't *you* let me in on your little secret? Who made you God?'

'She didn't want you to know Kit,' he responds carefully, 'She didn't want to worry you.'

'That wasn't her choice to make,' I cry, anguish invading every cell of my body, 'And it wasn't yours. I'm not a child. How dare you both keep me in the dark about something as important as this? Who the hell do you think you are Jason Buchannan?'

I'm vaguely aware that the tears are streaming down my face. 'I need to go to her now.'

'Kit.' Jason puts his hands on my shoulders and shakes me. 'Listen to me. She doesn't want you there. She has Neil. And nobody is saying she's going to die. You know what your aunt's like – she's a free spirit, and she values her own independence more than anything – that is, anything, except you.

'Look at me Kit,' he continues taking hold of my chin and turning my face to his.

'She. Does. Not. Want. You. To. See. Her. Like. This.' He punctuates each word.

'So why did she tell you then?' I ask finally, my voice a monotone in contrast to my early histrionics. Jason sighs, running his fingers through his hair in frustration, then he pulls me into his arms, ignoring my resistance.

'You've read the letter. She wanted to make sure you'd be

looked after sweetheart,' he murmurs. 'She knows I'll take care of you, no matter what happens.'

I pull away, saying harshly, 'Don't patronize me. I don't need you to take care of me, I don't need anyone to. I'm perfectly able to take care of myself.

'When my aunt comes back to Dartmouth, I'll be there waiting for her.' I pause, feeling the anger churn in my gut, and lean forward, declaring heatedly, 'I will be there Jason, whatever you or she has to say about it.'

Jason frowns at me. 'What exactly does that mean?' he questions in a low voice.

'It means you should have told me. It means you had no right to decide what's best for me. It means that I *will* take care of the woman who's been more than a mother to me, and it means that I'll never *ever* leave her.'

'Don't you understand Kit?' he says, his expression earnest and serious, 'She doesn't want that. She wants you to be free, to live your life,'

'I can't leave her Jason, and I won't,' I say resolutely, turning away from him and standing up.

'You wouldn't be leaving her straight away,' he argues fiercely, 'It will be months before this place is habitable, and your aunt will be back on her feet by then.'

I stare at him for a second then shake my head, crying, 'Why can't you see it? 'How can I simply abandon her when she needs me most?'

'You wouldn't be abandoning her,' he shouts in frustration. 'Flo doesn't want you to sacrifice your life for hers. You know it Kit. In your heart you know I'm right. Your aunt can come and live here if that's what she wants – she knows she'll always be welcome.'

I stare at his anguished features for a second, then harden my heart. 'Aunt Flo will never live anywhere else but Dartmouth,' I say finally, unemotionally, 'And neither will I.'

'So that's it then. You've made your decision.' His voice is tight and controlled and I feel him withdraw from me as he turns back into the knob, closing himself off.

'I won't walk away from her when she needs me Jason,' I repeat grimly. 'I won't ask you to understand, but the fact is, I owe her everything, I owe her my life.'

'Is that really what it's all about Kit?' he demands coldly, 'Or is this the excuse you've been waiting for?'

I stare at him, not knowing how to answer. What's the point in telling him I'd made the decision to stay? That I was going to tell him my home was wherever he was? The man in front of me is not the person I thought I'd be sharing my life with. I don't know who he is.

'I'll let you get a shower,' I answer bleakly instead, 'Then I'll pack my things and leave.'

He stares at me for a second, his beautiful eyes hooded and distant, then nods his head stiffly. 'As you wish. Perhaps you should speak to your friends before you go. They might not wish to stay here without y....' Before he can finish, there's a loud knocking on the bedroom door.

Without looking at me, Jason strides to the door and throws it open. Noah is standing on the other side looking serious.

'Have you heard from my father?'

'No, Jimmy just called. Hugo's fine Jason. It's the Admiral, he's had a heart attack.'

Chapter Fourteen

'What in God's name are you doing in Portsmouth James Eugene Noon?'

Eugene...? We're all sitting in the Great Hall unashamedly eavesdropping while Emily tears a strip off her husband. Even though she's standing by the main doors, which is the only place to get a signal, we can all hear her perfectly clearly.

I'm attempting to comfort Tory and Mabel while Noah's on the landline, frantically trying to book seats on the next flight down to Southampton.

Jason keeps going outside, trying to get hold of his father, but so far Hugo's mobile is still switched off.

Tory's managed to get through to the hospital and it seems that her father is currently in a stable condition but further surgery may well be needed if he pulls through the night.

Aileen's answer to everything bless her, is to keep supplying us with tea and shortbread, which she does very efficiently while mumbling, 'Tatties o'wer side and no mistake.' I remember her saying something similar the last time we were at Bloodstone Tower. Is there a disturbing pattern here?

There's no sign of Nicole for which I'm profoundly grateful.

'Have you managed to get us a flight?' Tory asks tearfully as Noah puts down the phone. 'There aren't any flights from Glasgow today, so I've booked us a private jet. We have to be at the airport in two hours, so get your skates on ladies and gents.' I look over at Jason who's just returned from outside in time to hear Noah's announcement.

'Do you have enough room for all of us?' he asks tightly

'We're not leaving anybody behind,' Noah answers decisively, 'Even Dotty...'

Well it has to be said, it's been a hell of a day. We arrived down in Southampton by lunch time and were at the hospital in Portsmouth for early afternoon. It really is amazing what an unlimited budget can get you.

What it can't get you of course, is your health. It was a shock to see the Admiral lying motionless in his hospital bed. I don't think I've ever seen him so still. In fact it didn't really look like him at all.

The only people allowed in the hospital room were Tory, Mabel and Noah, so I busied myself looking after Isaac and tried not to think about my aunt's impending operation, the possibility of Tory's father dying, or my break up with Jason. The last especially was pretty difficult when he was sitting a mere few feet away. Emily and Jimmy were also waiting – on opposite sides of the room. Their silence spoke volumes. Jimmy simply looked stricken. I'm sure he thought his old friend was pretty much indestructible.

Half way through the afternoon Jason finally managed to get hold of his father, and being privy to the one-sided conversation that ensued, I think I can safely say Hugo won't be adding another adventure to his bucket list any time soon. He claimed they'd come to Portsmouth so that he could attend a reunion dinner at HMS Nelson. On the face of it, totally credible. But I could tell that Jason wasn't buying it and would be demanding full disclosure when they met at our hotel later...

He saved the news about the Admiral until last, and I could tell from the way Jason's voice softened that it hit Hugo hard. It sounded as though he wanted to come straight to the hospital but Jason persuaded him – in a far gentler tone than before – to wait for us at the hotel.

I took a bit of time out to call Freddy. It almost feels as though my business back in Dartmouth is part of someone else's life, but a few seconds speaking to my second best friend brought it all flooding back, a bit like a tsunami. Before I can tell him about everything that's happened, Freddy launches into a tirade he's obviously been storing up...

'Don't ever ask me to get involved in your professional life again Kit Davies – first chocolate penises, then Dracula's bloody burial chamber. It's enough to put me off getting married altogether...'

It's heartening to know that my burgeoning business is in capable hands...

We finally left the hospital at around six and headed back to the hotel Noah had booked for all of us. Needless to say it's dog friendly and both Pickles and Dotty spent a much more relaxing afternoon than the rest of us getting acquainted with the queen size bed.

Unfortunately, not being aware of our less than amicable break-up, Noah booked a double room for Jason and me. The plus (or minus, depending on how you look at it I suppose) is that there are two queen size beds in our room, so at least we're not going to be forced to share...

We don't speak as we get ready for dinner, and every time I look over at Jason, he looks like he did when I first knew him – remote and withdrawn. My heart feels as though it's been torn into a thousand pieces and I have no idea how to bridge the chasm between us. Perhaps there really is nothing else to say.

Just before we leave the room, Jason's mobile rings and I can tell by his glance towards me that it's Neil. After a short conversation, Jason hands the phone to me, murmuring, 'I think you should hear this.'

Aunt Flo is going to be okay. The operation was a success. I want to berate him for keeping me in the dark, but I'm too relieved. Promising faithfully to keep me in the loop from now on, Neil hangs up and I automatically turn to share my joy with Jason, only to find that he's gone.

It seems that Hugo Buchannan has a paramour. Apparently her name is Alice and they knew each other when they worked in HMS Collingwood together, over forty years ago. I can see his admission has completely taken the wind right out of Jason's sails, especially as it appears she pre-dates his mother...

If I'm making it sound too much like we're having a bit of a party, I can assure we're not. After Hugo's confession, the silences are lengthy and painful, punctuated mainly by Mabel's quiet sobbing. It's almost worse that Hugo looks in such rude health, like the stroke never happened. Perhaps that's what a night of wild sex does for you after being celibate for a couple of decades. I suspect it might be something I'll get to learn.

The next morning we all troop over to the hospital again, this time to much more positive news. The Admiral has come through the night and is scheduled for surgery this afternoon. He's much more lucid and demanding to see Hugo to find out how his friend's night on the tiles went. He's also insisting on seeing Jimmy. Both men are allowed in for a brief ten minutes.

We all crowd round the window that looks into the room, I suspect to see if we can eavesdrop on Hugo's confession. Instead we're treated to the sight of Jimmy breaking down, his head resting on his old friend's bed, while the Admiral holds the small man's hand tightly.

When they come out, Jimmy's eyes are red from crying, and without saying anything, Emily pulls her husband to her for a hug before taking him outside for a spot of air.

At lunchtime I decide to go back to the hotel. I want to call Neil for an update on Flo and I also need to touch base with Freddy again in case he has a heart attack of his own. Plus I thought I'd take Pickles and Dotty out for a walk. They've been incredibly well behaved over the last couple of days, but I think the spaniel especially has been bewildered by the absence of his master.

Of course the other bonus is that I am putting space between myself and Jason. Being close to him without the intimacy is cutting me in two. If Tory wasn't so pre-occupied with her father, she would be demanding to know what the hell is going on. As it is, I can feel Noah's eyes on me speculatively.

Arriving back at the hotel, I head to my room to phone Neil. Our conversation yesterday was a little short and I want to make sure Flo really is okay and it's not just more bullshit based on my aunt's misguided attempts to protect me.

'Your aunt is going to be fine Kit,' Neil assures me for the twentieth time. The operation was a complete success and she's as strong as an ox. Please try not to worry, and for God's sake don't tell her you've seen through her attempts to treat you like you're still ten.' Tearfully I promise not to drop him in it, but as I put the phone down, I wonder what she'll say when she knows Jason and I have finished. That's another thing I won't tell her – that her health is the reason for our split.

I think back to the awful argument with Jason yesterday, and I sigh. Lies and secrets, however well meaning, have a way of causing havoc with everyone, and here I am perpetuating them. Was Jason so wrong after all?

Determinedly putting the whole thing out of my mind, I head to Tory and Noah's room to pick up the two dogs. Both of them are gratifyingly ecstatic to see me, and yes I know it's cupboard love, but I'll take anything I can get at the moment. Clipping on their leashes and tucking some dog treats in the pocket of my jeans, I decide to postpone speaking with Freddy until I'm out walking.

Our hotel is situated close to Southsea beach, a long shingly stretch of sand that extends out from Old Portsmouth. As it's summer, dogs are not allowed on the beach itself, but there's a lovely large grassy area, aptly named Southsea Common adjacent to it – perfect for walking dogs.

Once we reach the Common, I let them both off the lead, and it really lifts my spirits to see them so happy, bounding about, playing and chasing each other.

Before I get the opportunity to call Freddy, and let's be honest,

I have been putting it off slightly – as much as I love him, and am truly grateful for his help, Freddy's tendencies towards the dramatic can be singularly wearing at times – my phone rings. Talk of the Devil, it's Freddy and call me clairvoyant, but somehow I don't think it's good news…

~*~

Of course, he wouldn't dream of telling Kit, but Freddy was actually enjoying himself. It might be a trifle unorthodox, but everyone really seemed to be getting into the swing of things.

He'd met the groom last night to go over some last minute details and once you got past the fake fangs, white pancake makeup and blood red lips, he seemed like a real stand up bloke. His name was Norman and he spoke with a broad Liverpudlian accent. He was actually about as far away from the image of a sexy vampire you could possibly get, and kept saying, 'Nice one,' to everything Freddy ticked off his list.

So, all in all Freddy wasn't as nervous as he thought he would be come their big day. He'd been up at the crack of dawn, checked and double checked that everyone was doing what they were supposed to be doing, and now all that remained was to get in character before heading up to the cemetery for the ceremony. Kit was absolutely right, he did love dressing up and while of course he didn't want to steal Norman's thunder, he had to admit, he made a damn good vampire.

He stared at his reflection before adding the final touches – the cape and the fangs. Unfortunately the latter were bloody uncomfortable and when he practiced speaking with them in, his words came out just like Kaa in Disney's version of *Jungle Book*, along with a mountain of spittle. Still, it wasn't like he was going to have to make a speech.

After glancing at his watch, he noted that he still had another hour and fifteen minutes before everything kicked off, so he decided to leave a bit early. He hadn't visited the cemetery yet, because Norman had assured him that everything was in hand, but it wouldn't hurt to go up and check before the guests started arriving.

Strolling in the early July sunshine to pick up his little Renault, at first he enjoyed the curious glances cast his way. However, his car was parked down by the river front, which was a bit of a hike from his flat. By the time he finally got there, he was sweating buckets and his make-up was starting to slide.

Getting into the driver's seat, he pulled down the mirror and groaned. His face was now covered in white patches that looked as though he'd got a bad case of leprosy. He rummaged around and found an old tissue and gave his face a bit of a dab. The result was pretty impressive actually – he now looked as though he'd been dug up. He chuckled to himself, thinking how impressed the wedding guests were going to be, and started the car.

Five minutes later he was parking up at Dartmouth's only cemetery. There was now only half an hour to the ceremony, so after congratulating himself on his ongoing planning skills, he climbed out of the car and made his way into the graveyard.

Entering through the arched gateway, he expected to spot the wedding party without too much difficulty – after all, a wedding's not something you see every day in a place like this. Glancing round, he couldn't spot anybody at first, and looking back at his watch, he frowned. Just over twenty minutes – he'd have thought that most of the guests would have been assembled by now.

He took out his mobile phone, and was just about to give Norman a quick call, when he spotted the wedding party by the eastern gate. Of course, he'd come in through the wrong entrance. Hitching up his cape, he hurried towards the group of people milling around. As he arrived, puffing and panting, he gave his best Vincent Price chuckle and apologized for not getting here sooner. 'I'm not kidding,' he joked looking for Norman, 'I'm sure I'd be late for my own funeral.'

All eyes turned to him and he briefly registered that the entire party was dressed in black, before a large woman standing a few feet away, screamed loudly and fainted...

~*~

'You've done *what*?' I hiss as I listen to Freddy's garbled account of what's just happened. 'Oh my God Freddy, what the bloody hell were you doing up at the cemetery anyway?'

'What d'you mean, what was I doing there? What the hell do you think I was doing there? I was doing your bloody job,' he hisses back. 'I know you said I didn't need to attend the ceremony, but I thought I'd check everything was running smoothly before heading over to the crypt for the reception.'

I squeeze my eyes shut in horror. 'The ceremony isn't in the town graveyard you dork,' I yell, eliciting a few disapproving stares from fellow dog walkers, 'It's in the pet cemetery over by the creek.'

'But... but, what about Norman's father Rupert? He's not buried in the pet cemetery is he?' Freddy was horrified

'No but his bloody *dog* Rupert is...'

I feel sick. Freddy assures me that no one at the funeral would ever be likely to recognize him again, and the minute he cottoned on to his mistake, he'd legged it back to his car and driven off before anyone got a chance to take his registration number.

I instruct him to head straight for the wedding breakfast at the crypt and to tell absolutely no one. With a bit of luck, it won't make the front page of the Dartmouth Gazette.

I cut the call and look around for Pickles and Dotty, thinking my life can't get any worse. Wrong.

After a few minutes frantically calling them both, I'm just about to call for back up, when I spot Dotty barrelling towards me with a large German Shepherd in tow. Pickles appears to be attempting to keep up from the rear.

I can't tell from this distance whether they're playing or not, but a few seconds later when Dotty launches herself at me from a distance of six feet, only inches away from the Shepherd's jaws, I have my answer. Snatching the little dog to me, I screech and lift her high in the air, just as the large dog jumps up at me, snarling and dribbling.

'DOWN BOY,' I yell, panicking. If this dog gets me on the ground, both Dotty and I are toast. Not daring to take my eyes off it, I vaguely hear someone shouting, 'Max,' in the background.

The Shepherd's nose is inches from mine, when suddenly the dog bends its head and starts sniffing round my crotch. 'What the fu…,' I gasp as it suddenly starts tugging on my jeans, slowly but surely dragging them down over my bottom. Both hands are taken up with a shaking Dotty and I'm forced to stand helplessly as 'Max' slowly but surely yanks the legs right down to my ankles, then begins nosing around in the pockets until he unearths the treats I put in there earlier.

By the time his owner finally puts in an appearance, I'm standing in my knickers with my jeans in shreds round my ankles, thanking my lucky stars that I'm not wearing a thong…

It's almost three o'clock by the time I get back to the hospital after having to leg it into the city centre to buy a new pair of jeans. As I arrive in the waiting room, I'm just about to recount my adventures, thinking it might lighten the mood, when I realize there's no sign of Jason or Hugo.

I look over at Tory and my heart lurches as she stares back at me in sympathy. 'They've gone Kit,' she says gently, 'I think Jason wanted to take his father home as soon as possible, hopefully this time to get some rest.'

I take a deep breath, trying to force back the tears that are threatening to spill at last. 'Did…did he leave a message for me?' I manage to ask finally. Tory sighs, handing Isaac over to Noah, then she stands and walks over to me, enfolding my resistant body in her arms. 'Yes he did Kitty Kat, he said, tell her to be happy.'

Chapter Fifteen

The Admiral's bypass surgery is a complete success, and after staying in Portsmouth for another three days, Noah drives us back to Dartmouth. That is, all of us but Jimmy who's decided to stay behind – with his wife's blessing – to make sure his oldest friend does exactly what the doctor orders.

It appears the tables have turned somewhat, and, as Tory emphatically stated, 'It will do the old goat the world of good to do as he's told for once in his life.'

Mabel was packed off to look after Pickles, after the Admiral stated she was as much use as a chocolate teapot. So romantic…

My aunt's also recovering from her surgery and Neil's hoping to bring her back to her cottage in a couple of weeks. He's been instructed to tell me that, 'Flo's come down with a bit of a bug, so she's decided to stay in London for an extra week.' I sigh when he tells me, but promise to keep up the pretence. When did my life become so complicated?

I've no sooner dumped my bags on the bed, when Freddy arrives with wine and chocolate and I surmise that Tory's already broken the news to him. Still, I'm glad of his company on my first night home in what seems like ages, and he does his usual good job of taking my mind off my woes, especially when he gleefully shows me the headline on the front page of yesterday's Gazette…

Did local dignitary attend his own funeral from beyond the grave?

Well at least the wedding breakfast went off without a hitch.

The crypt was suitably spooky and no one set themselves or anyone else alight with the multitude of candles. In fact, it actually sounds like everyone had a really fabulous time, so much so, the happy couple have asked Freddy to be a godfather for their first child.

And what about me after all my hard work putting everything together? Well, at least I got paid…

It's only when I'm in bed that my mind inevitably goes back to thinking about Jason. As I lie there, it suddenly occurs to me that I never actually told him about my father being alive. The reality of our split finally hits home with all the force of a sledgehammer.

With a gasp, I sit bolt upright, burying my face in my hands, teeth clenched against the indescribable pain of knowing that now I'll never get the opportunity to tell him anything ever again.

The next day I head over to Aunt Flo's cottage, ostensibly to make sure that everything is okay for her homecoming. Of course the reality is that I need to keep busy to stop myself from thinking. If I stay occupied and bury the pain deep enough, maybe it will stop.

As I drive towards her home overlooking Blackpool Sands, I can't help but reflect how funny it is that this time last week I was actually not sure that I wanted to stay with Jason if it meant going up to Scotland. How things can change in the space of a few days.

Now, the thought of life without him, even in somewhere as remote as the Outer bloody Hebrides, seems untenable. It just goes to prove the old saying, 'You never know what you've got until you haven't got it anymore.'

I turn into my aunt's driveway, chanting, 'Keep busy, keep busy,' to myself. The pain will fade, I know it will, and if I can just get through the next few months, Jason will be gone from Dartmouth forever. Coming to a stop, I rest my head on the steering wheel fighting back the tears that seem to be permanently threatening to spill over.

'For God's sake get a grip girl,' I admonish myself sternly, 'You need to think about Aunt Flo now. Helping her get better, being there for her when she needs you is the only thing that's important.'

Sighing, I get out of the car and go to let myself in. I have to push the front door hard to get it open due to the pile of mail that's slowly become wedged under the bottom. The cottage has that closed up smell to it and, after bending down to pick up the post, I decide to open a few windows to let in some air. Dumping the mail on the kitchen table, I go to unlock the French doors, throwing them wide open to let the summer breeze into the stuffy kitchen. Taking a deep breath I step onto the terrace, letting the beautiful view and the warmth of the sun slowly sooth my battered spirit.

I make myself a coffee to drink outside, and decide to take the post out with me to check if there is anything important I might need to tell Neil about. Of course I wouldn't dream of invading my aunt's privacy by reading her personal mail, but whenever she's gone away in the past, she's always asked me to go through her post and open up anything I think might be urgent.

Taking a sip of my coffee, I grimace and reflect that it would taste much better with a good slug of brandy in it. If only I wasn't driving. With a regretful sigh, I sit down and place the cup onto a small table before sorting through Aunt Flo's correspondence. After a couple of seconds it's clear that most of them are bills or mail drops. There are a couple of letters from various parts of the world – fan mail I assume. That leaves just one type written envelope with the post mark from Brighton.

Where my father lives...

~*~

'Bollocking hell Jimmy, when did you turn into a prissy nurse maid? If I'd known you were going to treat me like I'm on my last legs, I'd have sent you packing with the others.'

'It's for your own good Sir,' Jimmy responded with endless patience. You know it won't do you any good to have a glass of Port after your dinner. You need fluids, and not the alcoholic kind.'

'What about the iron?' muttered Charles Shackleford sullenly, 'I'm sure Port's full of the damn stuff. Much better than sticking pellets the size of bloody golf balls up my jacksie.' Jimmy winced, thanking his lucky stars that that particular task hadn't been designated to him.

It had to be said that Admiral Shackleford was not a good patient. As the days wore on, Jimmy found himself taking on more and more of the day to day care of his best friend after the Admiral managed to offend pretty much everyone working on the hospital ward. As a result, the medical staff tried to avoid their cantankerous patient whenever they could.

'Why can't you just be pleasant Sir?' Jimmy had asked after the third nurse he'd insulted walked out in a huff.

'Well she has got an arse the size of an aircraft hanger,' the Admiral responded petulantly.

'She might well have, but that doesn't give you the right to say it to her face,' the small man admonished him. 'These people have to take care of you, and you really aren't making their job any easier Sir.'

'Keeps 'em on their toes,' the Admiral retorted, clearly unrepentant.

Jimmy sighed. When he offered to stay and watch over his oldest friend, he hadn't envisaged that it would involve keeping the peace. He should have known better. He could only be grateful that old Scotty never actually ended up on the receiving end of the Admiral's brand of nursing care.

'Do you fancy a game of Uckers Sir?' he asked, trying to give the Admiral something else to think about. Tetchily the Admiral agreed, and for the next hour at least, peace reigned in the small hospital room. Of course the advantage of being obnoxious was that at least the one dishing out the obscenities tended to be put into isolation – which suited Charles Shackleford much better than having to hobnob with every Tom, Dick or Harry. It was worse than Piccadilly Circus in this damn ward.

When the Admiral's dinner finally arrived, they both stared at it in silence.

'Do they think I haven't got any bloody teeth?' the Admiral grumbled eventually after poking the suspicious looking green mush on the plate, which looked pretty much the same as the equally suspicious looking yellow mush he'd had yesterday. 'How the bloody hell do they expect me to get back on my feet on eating this?'

He plonked his fork down on the untouched plate. 'That's it Jimmy, I've had enough. Go and get me some fish and chips – and that's an order.'

Of course Jimmy could have refused, but to be fair, he didn't really blame the Admiral for wanting some proper grub. And fish and chips seemed a fair trade off for the glass of Port his old friend was asking for earlier. With a quick salute, he headed out to find the nearest fish and chip shop.

Left alone, the Admiral leaned back against his pillows wearily. Bloody hard keeping up the pretence that everything was ship shape, but then it was either that or accept an early visit to Davy Jones Locker, and he was buggered if he was going to end up there before old Scotty.

After a couple of minutes he realized he needed to use the bathroom. Sighing he pressed the buzzer. As much as he didn't like to admit it, he wasn't up to doing the necessaries on his own.

A few minutes later, a young spritely nurse who looked to the Admiral as though she'd just come out of nappies, came bustling in with the whole, 'How are we today,' bloody nonsense. The Admiral confined himself to a series of grunts as she helped him off the bed and they slowly made their way across the room and out into the corridor.

It took nearly five minutes to get to the bathroom dragging his drip, and all the while she kept up this inane chatter that the Admiral very quickly learned to tune out. As they painstakingly made their way towards the facilities, the Admiral looked around with interest to see if there were any newcomers.

Just as they passed the nurses' station, there came a loud beep indicating there was a problem with one of the patients. En masse, the nurses gossiping at the station, rushed towards a room near the end of the corridor, just before the toilet.

'Poor bugger,' the Admiral thought to himself, 'Wonder if whoever it is could be on their way out?' He had to admit that the environment he found himself in was particularly suited to maudlin introspection and he couldn't help but look through the window of the room as they passed.

There were half a dozen people crowded round the bed and he could just see a pale figure lying unmoving under the covers. Automatically, he glanced at the name on the door and stopped dead, frowning.

The name card said the patient's name was Luke Anderson. He stared back through the window resisting the nurse's efforts to move him on. Where had he heard that name before?

~*~

'Aunt Flo's been trying to find my father,' I blurt out brandishing the letter when Tory finally opens the door in answer to my almost hysterical banging. She frowns for a second, before ushering me inside and marching me to the drawing room.

Once I'm seated, she pours a large measure of brandy, puts it into my hand and simply says, 'Drink it.' After a second's hesitation, I do as she asks. I hate brandy, but as the liquor burns its way past my throat, it has the desired calming effect.

'Now tell me,' she continues when I finally draw a deep shuddering breath.

'This letter is from a firm of solicitors in Brighton,' I whisper, pointing at the innocuous piece of paper lying on the table, 'I think my aunt started asking questions when she saw an announcement in the obituary column of the Dartmouth Gazette early this year.'

I show her the newspaper cutting which I found inside the

envelope.

**Former Dartmouth resident Susan Anderson
(96) passed away peacefully
on January 4th 2016 at her home in Brighton.
She was pre-deceased by her husband
John who died in 2007, and
leaves behind the couple's only son, Luke.
The funeral will be held at All Saints
Church in Brighton on 28th January, followed
by a private burial.**

She looks back up at me without speaking, so I continue, 'According to this solicitor's letter, when my grandmother died, she left her substantial estate to her only son – my father. Apparently there was more than enough to get him the best care available in the area after he suffered the stroke that nearly killed him – you know, the one he had after being locked up for trying to murder my aunt,' I add with bitter sarcasm.

'Of course there's the slight problem that they don't know what happened to him after the will was read, so any blackmailing attempts my aunt has up her sleeve are doomed to failure...'

Still silent, Tory reaches for the letter, waving it in front of her to ask my permission. 'Be my guest,' I mutter, taking another large slug of brandy.

'So now the solicitors are asking if your aunt wishes to take her enquiries further?' she questions quietly when she's finished. I nod my head, before laughing harshly, 'And if they go ahead and get Brighton's answer to Sherlock Holmes involved, I stand to become a very rich woman. How's that for a bloody soap opera plot?'

Tory looks back at the letter. 'Have you called your aunt about this?' she asks, 'She's in London isn't she?'

I laugh again, but this time it turns into a sob, and my best friend reaches out her hand to clasp mine. 'Don't cry Kitty Kat,' she murmurs enfolding me in a warm hug, 'If Flo is trying to contact your idiot father, then it's purely because she wants what's best for you.'

'His millions you mean?' I answer callously. She shakes her head. 'Not just that. Of course she wants to make sure you'll be well provided for when she's gone, but she also knows you need closure Kit. You can't go on burying your head in the sand and pretend none of it ever happened. Your aunt understands that. Why don't you call her in London?'

'Because I can't,' I wail suddenly, making her jump at my outburst. Then despite my promise to say nothing of my aunt's illness, I tell Tory where she is.

Chapter Sixteen

By the time Jimmy got back from the fish and chip shop, having smuggled the elicit meal past the eagle eyed nurses, the Admiral could hardly contain himself. 'Bollocking hell Jimmy, where have you been? I could have died of starvation and been bloody cremated in the time you took to get me some decent scran.'

'Sorry Sir,' Jimmy responded mildly, as always, completely oblivious to his old friend's sarcasm. 'The nearest chip shop was over a mile away.'

He opened the packet up for the Admiral and the heavenly smell of salt and vinegar wafted into both their noses. The batter was definitely soggy, and they had to eat with their fingers, but the Admiral couldn't remember the last time he'd enjoyed a meal quite as much.

'Damn me, that was good,' the Admiral belched after they'd finished.

'Are you feeling okay Sir?' Jimmy asked apprehensively wrapping up the remains, worrying that he'd been a bit too lax allowing his patient to eat such a huge portion.

'No good shutting the gate after the horse has bolted,' the Admiral gestured to the empty cartons. 'If a packet of fish and chips is enough to finish me off, then I'm bloody doomed Jimmy lad. I'm certainly not going to live the rest of my bollocking natural surviving on bunny grub.' Jimmy opened his mouth to say something else, but before he got the chance to speak, the Admiral interrupted with an excited gleam in his eyes that made Jimmy's heart sink into his boots.

'Listen Jimmy boy,' he whispered leaning forward, 'I want you to do a bit o' snooping for me.'

Jimmy frowned. 'Snooping?' he questioned, 'I don't like the sound of that Sir. Snooping and sticking our noses where they don't belong is what's caused nearly all our problems in the first place.'

'Don't be such a bloody nancy,' the Admiral went on, unperturbed. 'Just think of it as a bit of a recce.' The small man frowned again, clearly unconvinced.

'There's a bloke in a private room like this one, up near the heads,' Charles Shackleford continued, completely ignoring his friend's lacklustre reaction. The name on the door reads Luke Anderson. That ring any bells?' Jimmy shook his head mutely and the Admiral sighed, 'That's why you never got to be an officer Jimmy boy,' he muttered, 'No powers of observation.

'Luke Anderson. That was the name of the bloke Flo ran off to America with – Kit's old man. Jimmy frowned in confusion. 'But I thought he died, you know when Flo... er...'

'Blew his head off, I know,' the Admiral butted in, 'But did she actually *say* he was dead, or did we just assume it?'

'Well, if she blew his head off, I very much doubt he's still alive,' Jimmy responded matter of factly, trying his damndest to put a lid on his friend's latest bout of meddling. 'There must be hundreds if not thousands of Luke Andersons out there.' He waved in the general direction of the unknown man's room, 'He's very unlikely to be *the* Luke Anderson.'

'That as may be Jimmy lad.' The Admiral refused to be put off, 'But I would be derelict in my duty to my daughter's best friend if I didn't find out for sure.'

'But you're not going to be the one finding out Sir,' Jimmy grumbled in exasperation, 'It'll be me who gets caught nosing around. And anyway, what makes you think that Kit will want to know that her old man – who was clearly bonkers – is still alive anyway?'

The Admiral frowned, clearly not having thought of that.

Then he brightened, 'Closure Jimmy, closure. Always good for the soul.'

Jimmy sighed and the Admiral could see he wasn't convinced, so he tried another tack. 'If he does turn out to be her old man, we don't actually have to tell her if you think it's best not to, but I think we'd be remiss Jimmy boy if we didn't find out the whole truth.'

Of course this little speech moved his friend not one jot and Jimmy shook his head, before stating firmly, 'You're forgetting how well I know you Sir. This is me you're talking to. You don't want to know for anybody else's benefit but your own. You just enjoy being nosy.'

The Admiral adopted a wounded expression. 'I don't know how you can say such a thing Jimmy. Just look how much good I've done over the past two years. My daughter's married to the man of her dreams...'

'...And her best friend found out that her father was a murdering psychopath, and the person she thought was her aunt, was just a murderer.'

'That had nothing to do with me,' the Admiral protested indignantly, 'That was Flo's bloody skeleton, not mine.'

'But if you hadn't involved old Bible Basher Boris in the nuptials, poor Kit might still have been none the wiser.'

'So,' the Admiral leaned forward eagerly, 'Don't you think it's a good thing that we prove that her aunt... that Flo - isn't *actually* a cold blooded killer...?'

Jimmy opened his mouth to argue some more, then shut it again without speaking, and, putting the final nail in the coffin, the Admiral leaned back with a small theatrical groan. After adopting an exhausted but stoic pose, he closed his eyes as if the weight of keeping them open was simply too much.

After about thirty seconds, Jimmy exhaled noisily and the Admiral knew he'd won. With what appeared to be monumental effort, he opened his eyes and regarded his friend sadly.

'Give it a rest Sir,' Jimmy grumbled irritably, 'Your hangdog expression won't wash with anyone who knows you well.'

'But you'll do it?' the large man said, unashamedly abandoning the woe is me tactic.

'Yes I'll do it, but if I can't find anything out within ten minutes...'

'We'll abort the mission,' interrupted the Admiral excitedly.

In the event it was early afternoon of the next day before they were able to put their (or rather the Admiral's) plan into operation. Before he left the night before, Jimmy had been given explicit instructions to find the nearest fancy dress shop and buy himself a fake doctor's uniform and stethoscope. Consequently Jimmy found himself trawling old Portsmouth after breakfast in search of a costume shop.

Unfortunately, when he finally found the place he was looking for, the only white coat they had was clearly meant for a woman. It had a big pink heart on the front, with the words, *'Cute enough to stop your heart, and skilled enough to re-start It,'* splashed over the top. Of course, it was also slightly on the small size. Still, it came with the required fake stethoscope so Jimmy paid the rental fee and hurried back to the hospital.

'You can't wear that,' the Admiral spluttered when Jimmy tried the coat on in his friend's room, 'They'll never let you anywhere near Luke Anderson's room.'

'It was all I could get,' Jimmy responded firmly, hoping that his costume cock up would convince his friend to abort the mission. The Admiral sighed, and obviously reluctant to abandon his plan, stared thoughtfully at the small man in front of him. 'Just pick up my chart at the end of the bed and hold it in front of you,' he instructed at length.

Unfortunately for Jimmy, when he held the clipboard close to his chest, the heart motive was almost completely covered up and the Admiral nodded in satisfaction. 'That'll do Jimmy lad, just keep that chart close to your chest, hang your stethoscope round your neck and Bob's your Auntie - they won't be able to tell you apart from the real thing.' He glanced over at the door. 'We'll wait until they're bringing round the tea and biscuits at fifteen hundred hours – I've noticed that's when a lot of 'em scarper for a crafty fag or whatever – then we'll initiate the mission. Let's synchronize watches Jimmy boy.'

'I'm in the same room as you Sir,' Jimmy responded tetchily, wondering for the umpteenth time, how the bloody hell he always let himself get involved in the Admiral's harebrained schemes.

The Admiral narrowed his eyes. If time hadn't been of the essence, he would have been tempted to fine his former Master at Arms for insubordination. Instead he contented himself with The Look, which had the desired effect.

'Fourteen fifty two, by my watch Sir,' Jimmy said, saluting smartly. The Admiral looked down at his own watch. Unfortunately he wasn't wearing his glasses so could just about make out the actual face. 'Near enough,' he muttered after a couple of seconds squinting. Then looking back up, he thought he'd better get on with the obligatory pep talk.

'You've got just over five minutes to get yourself in character Jimmy. You're Doctor Noon now if anybody asks. You need to stride down that corridor like you own the place. You can do it lad, you were always good at acting.' Jimmy opened his mouth but before he could speak, the Admiral ploughed on, 'Think about what you're looking for Jimmy. We need to know who this bloke is, where he comes from, how old he is – all that malarkey.

'If he wakes up, ask him a couple of questions.' Jimmy raised his eyebrows, alarmed at the idea of actually having to speak to the patient. 'What kind of questions Sir?' he asked faintly.

The Admiral sighed. Why was it he always ended up with lily livered subordinates with no bloody back bone? 'I'm sure you'll think of something,' he said at length, 'Now stop bloody pussy footing around and get yourself out there.'

Seeing that any further argument would be futile, and secretly a little worried about his friend's pale drawn features, Jimmy capitulated with as much good grace as he could muster. Carefully clasping the chart to cover up most of the pink heart, he walked to the door and poked his head out into the corridor.

He could that see the nurses' station to the right was currently unoccupied. It was only a few yards, but it might as well have been a hundred. Taking a deep breath, he stepped out into the corridor and began walking purposefully, if slightly unsteadily, towards the station, and beyond that, his destination.

In the end, it was much easier than he'd anticipated. There were a couple of hairy seconds when the tea trolley trundled past, but no one paid him any real attention. Emboldened by his success, he strode confidently up to Mr. Anderson's room and peered in through the window. All clear.

Opening the door quietly, he tiptoed towards the bed. Despite the Admiral's instructions, he really didn't want to have to ask their quarry any questions. Laying his own clipboard carefully on the bottom of the bed, he picked up the patient's chart and, heart thumping, glanced through it.

Unfortunately, in the tradition of doctors everywhere, the information was completely illegible to anyone not familiar with this particular consultant's short hand. Squinting, Jimmy tried turning the chart upside down to see if that made any difference. He thought he managed to decipher the man's date of birth, which would make him about the right age, but that was about it. There appeared to be rather a lot of information underlined and in red, which Jimmy took to be less than positive and the patient himself didn't look as though he was long for this world.

Putting the chart back, Jimmy picked up his own clipboard and crept round the side of the bed. Feeling like a complete cad, he carefully opened the drawer of the bedside table, hoping to find some sort of clue in the patient's belongings. However, there was nothing – just a pair of glasses and a couple of handkerchiefs.

Sighing, he admitted defeat and silently closed the drawer. Turning towards the door, he took one last glance down at the still man in the bed.

Whose eyes were now open and regarding him steadily.

~*~

Despite Tory's assurances that closure would be good for me, it doesn't feel that way. To be fair, the ongoing problem with my absent father is currently vying for first place with ongoing visions of Jason in various states of undress with Aileen's pretty red haired niece.

In the last twenty four hours I can honestly say that there is no carnal position or situation that I haven't imagined them in. Consequently I'm knackered, irritable, and filled with the most awful conviction that I've made the worst decision of my life. Then of course I go on to think about how much I owe my aunt, how much she loves and needs me, and I come full circle. It's a never ending cycle of self torture and self loathing.

I can't help but compare my situation with that of Tory's when she misguidedly ended her relationship with Noah. Am I the same kind of stupid? Do the pair of us have some kind of masochistic need to be miserable? I shake my head. If we do, then Tory's managed to get over her addiction, and my reasoning for walking away from the man I've realized too late is the love of my life, is categorically different from hers – isn't it?

For the umpteenth time I glance down at my mobile phone. I'm not sure exactly what I'm hoping for. Jason did the smart thing when he walked away. Any contact now would just be prolonging the agony.

Sighing, I look down at my filofax. Hopefully if I throw myself into my work, the pain will start to fade. Aunt Flo should be back next week, so my parental issues could well be sorted – especially if daddy dearest has popped his clogs already – that would solve a lot of problems...

Sometimes I just hate my internal monologue. When did I become so bitter?

Suddenly my mobile rings and unable to stop my heart from lurching hopefully, I pick it up and stare at the caller's name, as hope slowly turns to confusion.

It's the Admiral.

Chapter Seventeen

J immy stared back at the silent man on the bed, then did the only thing that came into his head. He scarpered.

Once back out in the corridor, he stopped, sighing with relief. Any more of these close calls and they'd be putting him in the bed next door to the Admiral.

'There you are.' A strident voice cut into his reverie and he looked up in alarm to see a large woman dressed in green scrubs striding towards him. Staring at her mutely, it took a second to notice that she was pointing at the large pink heart on the front of his white coat. His heart stuttered in horror as he realized that he'd left the Admiral's medical chart in Luke Anderson's room.

'I can't say you're exactly what we were expecting.' She gazed at him, disapproval warring with disappointment. 'Can't believe they charged us a hundred quid, but then maybe older ladies nowadays like them small and dumpy.' When Jimmy still didn't speak, she shook her head and continued, 'Oh well, as you're all ready to go, we can head straight down to Mrs. Brown's room.'

Grabbing hold of Jimmy's arm, she propelled him towards the lift at the end of the corridor. Wordlessly, Jimmy allowed himself to be manhandled into the large elevator which was mercifully empty apart from the two of them.

As the doors closed, he shut his eyes, waiting for the inevitable denunciation and a declaration to call the police for attempting to impersonate a doctor. After a couple of seconds when no words were spoken, condemnatory or otherwise, he opened his eyes cautiously to find the nurse regarding at him with a bemused frown.

'How long have you been a stripper?' she asked curiously, 'I mean, do you still get a lot of business? Is it mostly from elderly women?'

Struck dumb, Jimmy simply stared at the nurse. She was obviously waiting for an answer and the lift was taking forever to move between floors. Licking his lips, Jimmy coughed and wondered hysterically what the bloody hell he was going to say.

'I..I...' was all he managed to force out, and unexpectedly she smiled. 'You know it's actually a really good idea. Mature women don't like to be intimidated by these young muscle men types. Employing cuddlier men who're getting on in years is a pretty smart move I'd say.' At her words, Jimmy shut his mouth again, and leaned back against the wall of the lift, trying to exude the charisma of a sexy pensioner. Unfortunately, resting his bottom on the handle bar played havoc with his piles, completely ruining his geriatric James Dean impression.

Luckily, before the nurse could ask any more questions, the doors opened. 'Here we are,' she announced cheerfully, 'Do you need to use the bathroom before you start?' Jimmy nodded his head enthusiastically and the nurse chuckled as she pointed out the men's loos.

'I'll go and make sure Mrs. Brown is ready for you. It's the second room on the left. We wouldn't want her to have a heart attack on her ninetieth birthday would we?'

Jimmy joined in her ribald laughter, even giving his hips a little suggestive wiggle, which definitely encouraged her to hurry off up the corridor. Then, as soon as the nurse entered Mrs. Brown's room, he turned and ran for the stairs.

It took Jimmy another ten minutes to find his way back to the Admiral's room after ditching his disguise in an unlocked storage cupboard. There was nothing he could do about the abandoned medical chart. Hopefully they'd think a nurse had mistakenly left it there.

After a few wrong turns, he finally found the correct room and burst in, slamming the door behind him and panting against it with relief.

The Admiral was so startled at his friend's sudden appearance, he sloshed his tea down his pyjamas. 'Bloody hell Jimmy,' he muttered, 'Are you trying to finish me off or what?'

'Sorry Sir,' Jimmy wheezed, glancing anxiously through the window in the door, 'It's just... well, I nearly got caught.' The Admiral shook his head in exasperation, and raised his cup towards his mouth once more.

'They mistook me for a stripper.'

The rest of the tea ended up on his ham sandwich.

By the time Jimmy had finished the whole story, he was unsure whether his old friend was silent because he couldn't believe anyone could possibly mistake him for a stripper, or because he was busy formulating a business plan...

In the end, however, the Admiral obviously remembered why Jimmy had been sneaking around in the first place, and gave a long sigh. 'Bloody shame we couldn't get to the bottom of the mystery Jimmy lad,' he grumbled, leaning back against his pillows.

'Oh no Sir, we've definitely solved the mystery,' Jimmy disagreed, 'When the chap opened his eyes and looked at me, I couldn't help but notice his eyes were emerald green, exactly like his daughter's.

'Our Luke Anderson is unquestionably Kit's father.'

~*~

Somehow it doesn't seem strange at all that the Admiral should be the one to unearth my father. Who needs private detectives when you've got Charles Shackleford and Jimmy Noon on the case?

I wonder if Tory's father will ever manage to actually get over his need to snoop. I can't see it happening any time soon.

So, if we backtrack slightly - somehow, the Admiral spotted that a very ill man on the same hospital floor as himself just happened to be related to his daughter's best friend. A man who hitherto (we think) had been residing somewhere in Brighton, nearly fifty miles away. You've really got to hand it to Tory's father, he never misses a trick.

The question is of course, what to do about it? Do I actually want to see my father? This is the man who was responsible for my mother's death and who tried to kill my aunt. But then, by all accounts he's extremely ill. So much so, that if I don't make a decision pretty soon, it's going to be a moot point anyway.

Has he changed at all? Does he regret his actions? These thoughts are going round and round in my head until I think I'll go as bonkers as he is from it all.

And then there's the kicker – does my father actually want to see me?

In the end, Tory convinces me to let Noah make some enquiries and it looks as though he's found someone to do an initial investigation. It all feels a bit Mike Hammerish really and I've spent the last couple of hours on their sofa chewing my finger nails.

I know I should be focusing on my business right now, but come on, the sudden discovery of a previously shadowy father, potentially on his last legs, doesn't happen often. Anyone would be forgiven for finding it a little difficult to concentrate on the more mundane matters of putting food on the table.

At least there's one good thing – this has certainly put the whole Jason fiasco on the back burner.

The front door bell rings and a few seconds later Freddy pops his head through the door. 'I heard the whereabouts of your nutty parent has possibly been discovered. Now that's something I couldn't miss.'

'You're such a caring, sensitive soul Freddy, what on earth would I do without you?' I mutter, barely looking up from a detailed inspection of my cuticles.

'You're right, I am,' he pronounced, plonking himself next to me, 'And better still, I've brought you a spot of wee fizz.' He waves a bottle of Prosecco under my nose. 'It's chilled beautifully, and of course, it's almost Champagne so you're allowed to have it for breakfast.'

Without asking if I actually want any, Tory goes to fetch glasses. I can't help but notice she's brought three. I guess I'm not the only one who's had a difficult few days. She also brings in a large bowl of crisps – perfect brunch fodder...

I take a handful of crisps and toss a couple on the floor for Dotty who's practically standing on her head in an effort to be noticed. Then I glance over at Noah's study. Tory's husband has been closeted in there for the last half an hour and I can hear the murmur of voices, so he's definitely speaking to someone.

Of course it might be nothing to do with my family tree, seeing as he is the world's most famous actor, but I'm having to fight the compulsion to go and listen at the door.

A sudden noise from Isaac's baby monitor causes us all to stop chomping for a second, but it's a false alarm.

Then suddenly the study door opens.

'The ball's in your court now Kit,' Noah says solemnly, 'Your father's indicated he wants to see you.'

~*~

My hands are clammy and my stomach is roiling uncomfortably as I stand outside my father's hospital room. Part of me feels as though I've cheated my aunt by coming here, but then she's been trying to trace him for months. Still, should I have told her I was coming?

No. Suddenly I'm sure. This is something I need to do by myself.

Tory came over to Portsmouth with me, but now I've left her and little Isaac to keep the Admiral out of trouble. Apparently, he was hauled over the coals when his medical chart was found in my father's room. I haven't asked how it actually got there.

So now I'm alone. The doctor has given permission for me to see my dad, but with a warning not to stay too long. With trepidation, I pull down the handle and open the door.

The air inside the room smells stale, the whole atmosphere permeated with the sickness of the man on the bed. For a second I think he's asleep, and cowardly I want to use it as an excuse to run back out. But then I see his eyes are open. Eyes just like mine. Staring straight at me.

Slowly, hesitantly, I walk towards the side of the bed. His eyes track me, but he doesn't speak, and I can't help but wonder if he can.

Then I arrive at the head of the bed and I look down at his frail arms lying on top of the covers, spider like fingers clenching and unclenching the cotton sheet.

'Hello dad.' My whisper comes out more like a croak and I keep my eyes firmly on his hands scrunching the coverlet.

'They tell me your name is Kit. Is that short for something?' His voice when it finally comes is dry and papery, almost too low to hear. I force my gaze up to meet his and I shake my head. 'It's always been Kit.'

Silence. I have no idea what to say. The man on the bed is a stranger to me. I realize that I thought there would be some kind of inherent recognition. Some sense of belonging – even if he had been the worst possible father anyone could ever wish for. How stupid is that?

Then suddenly his hand moves, fingers grasping mine in a surprisingly strong grip. So strong in fact that I panic, abruptly afraid that I won't be able to free myself. White hot fear shoots down my spine as I try unsuccessfully to pull my hand away.

'Is Florence still alive?' he rasps hoarsely. I nod my head and he relaxes his grip with a sigh. I snatch my hand away and ridiculously hold it behind my back. I know he can see my revulsion and I'm sorry for it. He closes his eyes with a low groan and I bend forward, abruptly afraid he might actually die here and now. As I lean closer, my heart flips as I see tears begin leaking from beneath his closed lids. I look around for a tissue, suddenly feeling as though I've fallen down a rabbit hole. His voice, when it comes, stops me in my tracks.

'I'm so sorry,' he whispers huskily, 'For everything. I don't ask you to forgive me, but I want you to know that my madness has passed. Please tell Florence...,' he swallows convulsively, and I reach for a glass of water to give him. Waving it away, he continues croakily, 'Tell Florence that if I could turn back the clock I would do so gladly.'

I stare at him silently. What am I supposed to say? Should I tell a dying man that I forgive him? The truth is, he's too much of an alien to me. I don't hate him. I don't actually feel anything at all for this stranger on the bed. I become aware that he's speaking again.

'I'm leaving everything I have to you of course.' I open my mouth to interrupt, but he holds his hand up weakly. 'I'm sure you don't want any such reminder of your bastard of a father, but please understand, I need to do this. I need to atone in some small way for the misery I caused your mother and Florence... and ... you,' he finished wearily.

I hear the door behind me opening, and to my shame, my first thought is one of relief. I look down at my father's drawn waxy features as the voice behind me tells me it's time to leave. Taking a deep breath, I tell him I'll come again tomorrow, but he shakes his head slowly.

'No,' he whispers faintly. 'We have nothing else to say. Live your life Kit.' Then he closes his eyes and the nurse gently takes my arm to guide me out of the room.

Chapter Eighteen

Flo climbed out of the car wearily. Seven hours – a long journey after more than two weeks in hospital. Wincing slightly at Pepé's anxious wriggling, she let him jump to the ground. Two seconds later he was off, foraging in the undergrowth, obviously ecstatic to be back at their cottage.

Smiling, Florence looked towards her home. He wasn't the only one happy to be back. Slowly she made her way towards the entrance where Neil was already unlocking and pushing open the front door. She'd expected there to be a closed up smell. Instead she smelled fresh flowers and furniture polish. Kit had obviously been busy. Entering the kitchen, she caught sight of a note on the table held in place by a large plate of scones. Bending down, she read, *'Don't worry, I didn't bake them! Welcome home aunt Flo. I'll pop up to see you tomorrow.'*

Suspiciously, she glanced over at Neil. Kit was always thoughtful, but didn't usually leave treats when her aunt arrived home from her travels.

'You haven't said anything to Kit about my operation have you dear?' she asked worriedly.

'Of course not darling,' Neil responded mildly with a quick kiss on her cheek. Flo narrowed her eyes. His calm response didn't alleviate her fears at all. Gently he drew her towards the terrace, ignoring her frown. 'A bit of fresh air will do you good Flo. Sit down while I make us both a nice cup of tea.'

Florence snorted. 'Cup of tea be damned, you can fix me a large glass of wine. I haven't had a drink in three weeks.' Neil chuckled, knowing that telling her she wasn't supposed to drink would fall on deaf ears. If he gave in to her now, she would accept just the one glass. If he fought her over it, she'd more than likely drink the whole bottle, just to spite him.

Five minutes later they sat opposite one another in contented silence. Pepé had returned from his explorations and ensconced himself underneath his mistress's blanket, his favourite place in the whole world. Flo stroked the little dog absently, wondering how to broach the subject she'd been agonizing over for the whole journey.

In the end, she decided to just come out with it. Her first alcoholic drink in nearly a month might have had something to do with her bravado.

'I'm ready to get married now Neil.' Her voice was decisive, almost defiant and achieved the not so gratifying result of her agent choking on his wine.

Watching Neil splutter, Flo felt uncharacteristically uncertain. Was she wrong? Was marriage no longer on the cards?

Heart thumping she went on when his coughing had died down, 'I mean, you don't have to move here to Dartmouth if you don't want to. I'd be happy to move to London if that's what you'd prefer.' Her heart continued to hammer in the face of his silence. Then he looked up, and she could see tears glinting in his warm brown eyes.

Climbing to his feet, he walked over and kneeled in front of her. 'I'd live in the middle of the Sahara Desert if that was your requirement to marry me. Can we do it tomorrow in case you change your mind…?'

~*~

My father died three days ago.

I still don't know how I feel about it. The whole experience was very surreal. I didn't know him at all and yet I cried when I heard the news.

I've also been informed that I'm now a very rich woman – or

will be when all the formalities have been sorted out. How's that for bizarre. If Jason and I were still together, he wouldn't need Noah's money to renovate Bloodstone Tower.

Determinedly I force my mind away from Jason and on to my Aunt Flo who returned from her *little holiday in London* yesterday. I haven't told her about my father yet. I didn't want to do it over the phone. To be fair, I'm not sure how she'll react. I mean she loved him once upon a time, didn't she?

I'm intending to head up to her cottage as soon as I've finished some paperwork. She actually sounded a bit breathless when I spoke to her. She said she had something to tell me, which I hope means she's going to come clean about her illness. Of course, childishly, I wanted to say, 'I've got something to tell you too, and I bet my news is bigger than yours...' Obviously I didn't.

Normal service has definitely resumed at The Admiralty.

Tory's father came home a few days ago and is now being bossed about by both his wife and his daughter. Neither is allowing him to do anything at all, and in the last exasperated phone call I had from her this morning she told me he was threatening to throw himself into the River Dart if he didn't get out from under their bollocking feet pronto...

In the end they reached a compromise which consists of Jimmy coming over this afternoon to take the Admiral for a little drive – to the Ship Inn...

I look down at my accounts littering the table. The fact that I actually don't need to work anymore hasn't really sunk in yet. And anyway, what would I do instead? If I tried the same nursing approach as Tory and Mable with Aunt Flo, she'd probably throw me out. Helplessly my mind goes back to Jason and I wonder what he's doing now.

Tory tells me that his father is doing well, but she's not sure if that's because he has a pretty redhead taking care of him, or the fact that he and his old flame Alice seem to have become an item. Jason told Noah that she apparently thought the efforts his father went to in order to meet up with her were all very romantic. Of course the Admiral has claimed full responsibility for bringing them together...

Jason is actually due to come back to Dartmouth in a few weeks. The thought of seeing him again fills me alternately with dread and longing. It could be that he and the pretty redhead have become an item too. Tory hasn't said anything, and I'm too scared to ask her to find out.

Still, there is one really positive event on the horizon. Tory and Noah have decided to have little Isaac baptized, so I'm going to be able to make good my promise to the local printers – my conscience is now clear...

I was a bit surprised actually – neither of them are particularly religious, but apparently the Admiral is insisting that his grandson be raised Church of England in true naval tradition – you know, God Save the Queen and all that.

Of course it's not necessary to do the whole thing quite so soon, apart from the fact that they intend to ask Bible Basher Boris to do the honours – and there's no saying the old priest will be around in another twelve months...

I think they both felt more than a little guilty that they were so relieved when he'd been unable to officiate at their wedding last year. Mind you they've decided to do the service outside in their garden – partly because the weather has been perfect since we hit July, but mostly because having the whole thing outside seemed the safest way to ensure that all guests actually survive the ceremony...

With a sigh I finally give up on my paperwork. I might as well go up and see my aunt...

'I'm so sorry sweetie, I should have told you I was trying to trace your father. It was completely wrong of me to do it under your nose. It's just... well, I wanted to make sure you'll be alright if anything happens to me.'

'Well, now you know I'll be absolutely tickety-boo, so you don't have to worry anymore.'

I make no effort to dampen my caustic response to Aunt Flo's apology, feeling a sudden resurgence of anger as I remember her bloody letter to Jason. But when I see her bite her lip with anxiety, and remember that she's just come out of a major operation, I relent, leaning forward to give her a warm hug.

'It's okay Flo, really it is. I was sad when I heard about his death, but my father was a stranger to me. To be honest, I was more concerned about how you'd take it. He seemed genuinely remorseful over the awful things he'd done.'

'So he should have been.' Aunt Flo's comment matches mine for sharpness, stating exactly how she feels about her former lover.

'He ruined so many lives Kit,' she continues, shaking her head, 'I'm just happy he tried to do the right thing by you before he died. It's no more than you deserve darling.'

She returns my hug, then leans back and claps her hands. 'Let's talk about nicer things,' she declares with a smile. How's it going with that gorgeous man of yours?'

I open my mouth, not exactly sure what I'm going to say, but, before I can get my thoughts together, she leans back and laughs gaily, glancing over at Neil, who's been sitting quietly with Pepé on his lap. 'What?' I ask instead, looking backwards and forwards between the two of them.

'I've asked Neil to marry me,' she says happily, 'And he's accepted. We're going to divide our time between here and Neil's flat in London.'

I stare at her in shock. All I can think is that *she doesn't need me.* My heart slams against my ribs as I realize the truth. *She never needed me.* It was just my idiotic sense of duty and my ridiculous fear of change that made her into some kind of invalid who needed looking after. She was my excuse to run away. Jason was right on every count.

Realizing that they're both waiting for a response, I drag myself back to the present and smile broadly, throwing my arms around her. 'Congratulations, it's about bloody time,' I say sincerely as I look over her shoulder at Neil's huge grin. 'Have you decided when you're going to finally make an honest man of him?' I lean back to look into her joyful face.

'I think Neil's scared I might change my mind,' she chuckles, 'If he has his way, we'll be doing it next week. But I'd like a little more time to plan. After all, I've only been married once and that was a dismal clandestine affair. This time, I'd like to do it properly.'

She looks over at Neil, her eyes warm with love. 'We've waited such a long time – too long. And that was my fault, I know, but what are a few more weeks. It's not like we're ever going to do it again...'

Somehow I manage to get out of the cottage without actually telling her about my break-up with Jason. I kept the conversation firmly on my aunt and Neil, which wasn't too difficult. I've never seen my aunt so happy. We drank some bubbly and I skillfully evaded any questions about my former boyfriend.

As I walk to the car, my stomach is churning and a voice in my head is screaming, 'Idiot,' over and over again.

Driving back towards Dartmouth, my feelings alternate between misery and hope. Would he consider taking me back if I pluck up the courage to contact him? Should I wait for him to get back to Dartmouth, or call, or write a letter, or send a text, or... has he moved on?

I think back to the easy banter between him and Nicole. Aileen's niece obviously loves it in Scotland. It probably wouldn't take much persuasion to convince her to stay. I mean, who wouldn't fall over themselves to be part of such an exciting project with a bloody gorgeous man like Jason Buchannan? Only imbeciles like me...

Barely managing to stop myself from banging my head against the steering wheel in an agony of uncertainty and frustration, I decide that spending the evening alone isn't a good idea. I call Tory to see if they'll let me stay the night. My best friend acquiesces immediately as I knew she would. Of course the deal will be that I come clean, but come on, who else can I talk to?

An hour later I'm driving round the headland to Chez Westbrook armed with two bottles of plonk, a family size bag of crisps and a large tub of salted caramel ice-cream. Coming clean always works best with lots of carbohydrates...

Tory draws me into a big hug as I open the door. Then, without speaking, she turns and leads me through the drawing room and out onto the large terrace overlooking the river. 'Sit,' she commands, relieving me of my goodies before disappearing towards the kitchen.

I collapse with relief onto the large comfortable L-shaped sofa, positioned to make the most of the beautiful view, and allow myself to relax into the early evening warmth. Dotty snuggles up on my lap and a few minutes later Tory returns with a large tray laden with the requisite carbs. Placing a glass in front of me, she sits down and says, 'Spill.'

'What's with the one word sentences?' I grumble, not actually sure where to start. She stares at me, eyebrows raised. Stalling, I take a large gulp of my wine before asking, 'Where's Noah?'

'Putting Isaac to bed. Come on Kitty Kat, you didn't come here just to get trollied, and I'd like to know what's happened while you can still string a sentence together.'

Sighing, I stare out over the river, idly watching a yacht make its way out to sea. 'My aunt's getting married,' I say eventually, taking another large swig from my glass.

'That's wonderful news – isn't it?' Tory's response is slightly puzzled, and I realize that with everything that's happened, I've never really come clean about the actual reason Jason and I broke up. Oh, she knows I was balking against re-locating to Scotland, and she knows about my aunt's illness. But chances are she's not actually put together two and two together.

So I take a deep breath, and tell her...

Half way through, Noah arrives and sits down, silently helping himself to a drink and nibbles.

'So she never really needed me after all,' I conclude with a hiccupping sob, 'And now, I have no idea whether Jason will ever consider giving our relationship a second chance – especially as I was so against moving to Scotland in the first place.'

'Of course he will,' Tory exclaims heatedly, leaning forward to grip my hand. 'He loves you Kit, doesn't he Noah?'

In the silence that follows, you could have heard a pin drop. Frowning, Tory turns towards her husband. 'Jason loves her doesn't he,' she repeats, making her words a statement rather than a question.

Noah stares soberly at us both for a few seconds, then, running his hand through his hair, he shakes his head uncertainly. 'Truthfully? I don't know how Jason feels. He doesn't wear his heart on his sleeve as you well know, but I do know he's been talking about his housekeeper's niece an awful lot during our phone calls. I get the feeling that there may be more between them than simply employer and employee.

'I'm so sorry to be the bearer of bad news Kitty Kat, but I don't want you to raise your hopes up, only to have them dashed. Let me speak with Jason. I'll find out what I can.'

I stare at Noah stricken, irrationally hating him for putting my worst fears into words. I can see Tory glaring at him from the corner of my eye, but when she goes to speak, I grip her hand tightly.

'Noah's right,' I murmur, turning towards her, 'What would be the point of me blithely thinking that all will be well simply because I've changed my mind.

'When I last spoke with Jason, he was under no illusion that I would relent. Why on earth shouldn't he get on with his life?' I turn back towards Noah's unsmiling face, and the sympathy shining in his beautiful eyes, nearly causes me to break down.

'Please don't say anything to him Noah,' I manage to whisper around the lump in my throat, 'He deserves to be happy. He's moving on, and that's a good thing - I don't want you to rock the boat.'

Strangling the huge sob that seems determined to form in the back of my throat, I turn to the bottle of wine on the table, and clumsily slosh a large amount into my wine glass with the rest of it landing on Dotty's head. Holding the glass up by the stem, I mumble, 'Here's to moving on.'

'So, what will you do?' asks Tory softly, turning me back to face her.

'Do?' I question with a bleak smile, 'Right now, what I'm going to do is to get well and truly drunk...'

Chapter Nineteen

'**S**o what the bloody hell do you want me to do about it?' The Admiral's loud response was not helping Tory's temper. She looked around at the regulars in the Ship, all of whom were eavesdropping shamelessly. 'Could you at least try and keep your voice down?' she hissed, only narrowly resisting the urge to give him a swift kick on the shin.

'I think she wants you to make some enquiries Sir, you know, the kind of enquiries you're always so good at,' Jimmy muttered awkwardly. The small man was sitting on the other side of the Admiral and both of them were hugely uncomfortable with the turn of events.

The Ship Inn and Victory Shackleford did not go together. It was like one of those new fangled bloody ridiculous ideas of putting chilli in chocolate, or salt in caramel. Some things were never meant to be in the same space at the same time. And one of those things was Charles Shackleford's daughter frequenting her father's local. Bloody sacrilege.

The Admiral glared down at his pint, wondering if he stared at it long enough, she'd get fed up and leave. He should have known better.

'Why is it that the one time I actually *ask* you to interfere in something, you start acting all holier than thou and making excuses? I'm beginning to think you've gone soft since your heart attack.'

Without waiting for a reply, Tory climbed down from her seat, picked up Dotty from her comfortable position on Pickles' back and started towards the door. Just as she reached it, she turned back and delivered the punch line. 'I have to say I'm disappointed in you father. You're no longer the irresponsible meddlesome old windbag you once were.'

The whole pub was silent as the door slammed behind her. 'Bloody cheek,' muttered the Admiral as the conversation started up once more, 'I'm every bit as bollocking interfering as I ever was.'

'Yes you are Sir,' affirmed Jimmy passionately, his fervent tone earning him a suspicious look. However, the Admiral contented himself with a small nod of acknowledgement at his friend's insight and turned his mind back to the problem at hand. He had to confess to feeling a small frisson of excitement – a feeling that had been distinctly lacking since he'd come out of hospital. Maybe Victory was right, maybe he had gone soft.

He shook his head and turned to his friend with a sigh. 'It's no good Jimmy lad, as much as we might want to, we can't hang up our deerstalkers yet, the world needs us...

~*~

Tory's heart was still thudding uncomfortably when she arrived home. To her relief, Noah was still upstairs with Isaac. She'd vaguely told her husband that she was just popping down to the Ship to check on her father, but that excuse would collapse under any kind of hard questioning – she was a terrible liar. Hanging her coat up, Tory wondered what on earth she'd been thinking – actually encouraging the Admiral to stick his nose into affairs that were none of his business, but she couldn't think what else to do.

Noah had flatly refused to go against Kit's wishes and speak to Jason, which meant that she couldn't either. The only person who didn't give a rat's arse about anyone's wishes apart from his own was her father.

Tory simply couldn't believe that Jason would willingly walk away from her best friend. She'd seen how he looked at Kit – that kind of passion wasn't something that died over night.

Tory thought back to the break up between her and Noah. Her father had told her then that if she wanted the actor, she needed to get off her arse and go get him.

If Kit wasn't going to do that with Jason, then it was up to her best friend to take steps. She just hoped that Kit would forgive her if she ever found out…

~*~

The Admiral sat down in his favourite chair, a glass of Port on the table next to him. His study was the only place he was able to sneak a quick tipple of the hard stuff. His wife was like a blood hound. She could sniff out alcohol at fifty paces. He shook his head at the unfairness of his lot before turning his mind to the matter at hand. He needed to meet up with Jimmy pronto. The problem was he'd already exceeded his weekly allotted trips to the Ship and if he asked Jimmy to meet him here, there was no doubt Mabel would smell a bloody great rodent. He could of course enlist the help of Victory, since it was her fault he was reduced to looking for a way to sneak out of the bloody house in the first place.

'I'm popping over to Marks and Spencer's dear.' His wife's shout gave him a few seconds to hide his glass as her words preceded her entrance to his study. Did the woman have no bloody manners? A man's study was his sanctuary. Even Victory knew never to step over the threshold unless invited. But Mabel had no such restraint. It was a damn good job she could make a cracking steak and kidney pudding, or he might have been tempted to take steps…

'Did you hear what I said dear?' Mabel called again as she brazenly walked right in to his refuge. The Admiral could tell that her eyes were scanning the room for signs of anything untoward and he thanked his lucky stars that he'd had the foresight to put the chocolate coated peanuts in his back pocket.

'Of course dear,' he responded through gritted teeth. Mabel

stared at him for a second with narrowed eyes. The Admiral felt himself begin to sweat. The woman had some kind of bloody radar when it came to spotting his smuggled treats. So far she'd confiscated three family size bags of cheese and onion crisps, five sausage rolls and tin of Quality Street. Fortunately she hadn't yet discovered his secret stash of Cockburn's Special Reserve...

'Will you be long my dove?' As soon as the words were out of his mouth, the Admiral cursed his stupidity as Mabel halted her retreat and turned back to stare at him suspiciously. 'Why?' she asked guardedly.

Somehow he managed to keep his expression of polite interest as he sought to dig himself out of the hole. 'No reason sweetheart. I just thought I'd take Pickles for a bit of a walk up the lane – if you think that's acceptable of course my angel.'

Mabel's face softened, indicating he'd averted potential disaster. 'I'll be gone a couple of hours I should think. A bit of fresh air will do you good, just don't overdo it will you Charlie?'

'I wouldn't dream of it darling.' Damn, he'd overdone it, he could tell. But after a couple more seconds staring at him skeptically, she thankfully retreated and he sagged with relief.

Right, he'd got an hour and a half to get to the Ship and back. If he walked on the flat path along the river, he should be able to manage it easily. He went to his study door to listen, and as soon as he heard the door slam, he got straight on the phone to Jimmy.

By the time he arrived at the Ship, he'd got a bit of a sweat on. Even Pickles was puffing and panting. Still, he'd managed it, although it was a bit harder than usual - this bloody dieting lark wasn't doing him any good at all.

After taking a bit of breather, he pushed open the door and saw with approval that Jimmy was already ensconced at the bar and had his pint ready and waiting. He nodded to himself in satisfaction. Old Jimmy might have made the odd bid for freedom over the last couple of years, but good training would always win out.

Clambering onto the seat next to his former Master at Arms,

the Admiral took a long draft of his pint before saying anything. Unfortunately Jimmy got in there first.

'That's the only drink you're allowed Sir, so you might want to take it a bit slower.' After spluttering into his beer, the Admiral looked up at his friend incredulously. This was mutiny.

Before he could get a word in however, Jimmy held up his hand. 'It's not me Sir. Mabel's had a word with the barman. He's only supposed to serve you one alcoholic drink. He said you're allowed to have tonic water though if you're still a bit dry after your pint.'

For a second the Admiral stared at Jimmy in disbelief. How did Mabel know he was here? This was a bloody disaster - his wife could read him like a book. His whole life was in tatters and he felt like crying.

Jimmy put his hand on the Admiral's shoulder and patted it sympathetically, before leaning forward and whispering, 'Don't worry Sir, I've bought you a pickled egg instead...'

~*~

I'm determined that little Isaac's baptism will be a truly memorable occasion. I know it's only a christening, but I need to focus on something, and the couple of weddings I've got in the pipeline haven't been taking nearly enough of my time – or more importantly, my brain.

I have two weeks to bring it all together and I've spent the last two days poring over magazines and websites. There are going to be fifty guests and the invitations have gone out already – giving me even more brownie points with the printers...

At the moment, I can't decide whether a choir will be over the top. I bite the end of my pen doubtfully. Maybe I should call Freddy. He's pretty good at judging when something is too much. Then I think back to his penchant for red velvet at Tory and Noah's wedding. Maybe not.

Tory's given me complete carte blanche with the proviso that I use local people. So there aren't going to be any chocolate penises at this particular party...

In a moment of inspiration, I decide to check out the church to see if I can actually watch a baptism take place. The parish church is only round the corner from my flat, so it won't take me five minutes to find out if there are any christenings scheduled for this Sunday.

Just as I head out, my mobile rings, and glancing down I see Freddy's name come up on the screen. For a second I'm tempted to ignore it, but then of course there's a possibility he might ring again when I'm actually in the church. Swiping the front screen, I put the phone to my ear.

'I need to speak to you,' Freddy says breathlessly as soon as we're connected.

'Why what's up?' I ask a little apprehensively, sensing that Freddy's fondness for gossip is about to be given free rein.

'Not over the phone,' he answers showing unusual restraint. Usually he can't wait to pass on whatever rumour he's unearthed at the earliest opportunity. His self control only serves to increase the volume of the warning bells already clanging in my head.

'I'm heading round the corner to the parish church. You can meet me outside if you want,' I say in the calmest voice I can muster.

'Why the bloody hell are you going to church on a Thursday?' he asks, surprise temporarily sidetracking him.

'I don't usually go to church on a Sunday either Freddy,' I respond drily before sharing my brilliant idea. There's a short silence, then, 'Okay, I'll meet you at the gate, and after you've done your recce, we can go to the Cherub.'

The alarm bells are positively crashing round my head now. If Freddy thinks I need alcohol to hear whatever he has to tell me, then it's worse than I thought. Cutting the call, I hurry down the stairs, anxious now to get my fact finding mission over with. A few minutes later I arrive outside St Saviour's Church. There's no sign of Freddy yet, so I determinedly force my mind back to the matter at hand and begin scanning the parish notice board.

While reading, I become aware of a woman marching up the street towards me. Glancing round, it quickly becomes clear that she's very irate and is dragging a reluctant child by the hand. As she gets closer, my heart sinks as I recognize my nemesis from the wedding I arranged a few weeks ago. I have no idea who the woman is, but the child she's dragging is most definitely *Chardonnay*. I'd know that wailing anywhere.

'Where's the vicar?' she shouts over her charge's howling.

'Er, I'm not sure,' I respond uncertainly, stepping back. 'Is there something wrong?' I question, reluctantly.

'WRONG... WRONG... I'LL TELL YOU WHAT'S BLOODY WRONG. THIS LITTLE MADAM HERE TRIED TO SUPER GLUE MY POOR LITTLE ADRIAN'S FINGERS TO HIS RIGHT NOSTRIL.' The woman's voice could probably be heard all the way over to Kingswear.

'NO I DIDN'T,' yells *Chardonnay*, not to be outdone. 'IT WAS GOD WHO DONE IT SEEIN' AS ADRIAN'S ALWAYS GOT HIS FINGER UP HIS NOSE. HE'S DISGUSTIN.' The woman glares down at the unrepentant child before turning back to me, and thankfully lowering her tone, continues self righteously, 'I told her we'd come and ask the vicar if God would do such a terrible thing to a helpless boy.'

I become aware that we now have an interested group of spectators, including Freddy who I can see grinning out the corner of my eye. What is it about this bloody child that seems to attract an audience?

'Are you saying you didn't superglue Adrian's finger to his nose, er... young lady?' I ask sternly – mainly for want of something better to say and hoping against hope that someone has the sense to fetch the priest.

Chardonnay stares up at me and I can see the moment recognition enters her eyes.

'You're that lady with the chocolate willies,' she states emphatically and my heart sinks.

'They weren't *willies* exactly,' I protest, trying to cut her off at the pass.

'YES THEY WERE,' she yells, dropping back into megaphone mode. 'YOU 'AD A 'UNDRED CHOCOLATE WILLIES IN THE BACK OF YOUR CAR. YOU'RE DISGUSTIN' TOO...'

I glance around at the engrossed listeners. 'Now, that's not *strictly* true,' I say, protesting my innocence weakly.

This was clearly getting out of hand and I frantically look round for Freddy to extricate me, knowing that any excuse I give now for having a hundred chocolate penises in my car will simply add to the titillation of the rapt audience.

Luckily, at precisely that moment, the church gate opens and out comes the vicar. Thinking that now is probably not the time to ask him about forthcoming Christenings, I wave vaguely towards my nemesis and her vociferous jailor before doing a runner.

'My business is going to go down the pan after that little fiasco,' I mourn despondently while nursing my glass of wine fifteen minutes later.

'I can't believe you never actually told me about your debacle with the chocolate balloons,' Freddy states indignantly, 'And after all our hard work too.'

I shake my head sadly and take a sip of my wine, thinking back to my near disaster. So much for thinking outside the box.

'At least you didn't meet her mother Sharon,' I say with a shudder, 'She told me no bride would want a load of bollocks decorating the tables on her wedding day.'

We stare at each other for a second, then burst out laughing. 'Bloody hell, that's priceless,' Freddy snorts when we finally get ourselves under control. I nod my head, still giggling. 'So what was so important to tell me that it necessitated plying me with alcohol beforehand?' I question cheerfully.

Freddy's laughter slows down, then finally stops as he obviously remembers the reason for our meeting. My own mirth dies in response and I stare at him waiting.

After taking another gulp of his wine, he looks at me seriously. 'Jason sent me an email this morning. He says he's received a letter. Supposedly from you…'

Chapter Twenty

The Admiral had terrible wind. It was the bloody pickled egg, he knew it. If this carried on much longer, he'd be rivalling old Boris in the anal acoustic stakes.

Still, his meeting with Jimmy had gone according to plan, apart from the depressing knowledge that Mabel now seemed to be able to predict his every move. Of course, the only silver lining was the fact that his wife knew he was at the Ship, which meant that he didn't need to get back to the Admiralty before her. Consequently he and Jimmy were able to settle themselves in a corner and put together *Operation Bloodstone.* For once Jimmy didn't protest at their proposed involvement in Kit's love life and the Admiral was almost certain it was because the order had come from Victory.

So they sat and plotted together while surreptitiously sharing the pint Jimmy had bought for himself.

'The thing is Jimmy lad, we can't just up sticks and disappear up to Scotland again. That won't bloody wash with anyone, and as much as it grieves me to say it, young Buchannan is not likely to listen to anything we have to say.

'No Jimmy, the only way we're going to conduct a successful operation is to employ subterfuge.'

Jimmy nodded his head dutifully, and waited as the Admiral produced a large sheet of paper and a pen with a dramatic flourish.

'Jimmy my boy, we're going to write ourselves a love letter...'

~*~

'But I haven't written a letter to Jason,' I protest faintly. 'What does it say?'

Freddy takes out a sheet of paper he's obviously printed off from his computer and hands it to me with a grimace. 'Read it and weep,' he mumbles knocking back the rest of his wine.

Frowning, I open the piece of paper and begin to read...

Dearest darling Jason

I know I've behaved a bit like a snivelling nancy, but I want you to know that whatever happened between us is in the past.

Will you please forgive me? I can't possibly live without you and if that means coming to live in the pile of ruins you call home, then I'm game.

Tory says I'm a bit of a sad case and I need to get my arse in gear. She's right dear Jason. I can't think of anyone else I'd rather be with, even if it means abandoning my current post.

Please say you will come down to Dartmouth for a bit of a chat. I'm sure we can come to some sort of arrangement.

Furthermore, the Admiral told me about the bit of stuff you've got stashed away in Bloodstone Tower. Dearest Jason let me assure you with all my heart that the only bit of stuff you need is me, so please make sure you get rid of her before we shack up.

Your ever faithful Kit xxxxxxxx

I look up. 'Please tell me he doesn't really think I've written this,' I say hoarsely. 'I'm going to bloody kill Tory's old man...' I crumple the piece of paper viciously, imagining it's the Admiral's throat. 'But first you can get me another drink.'

An hour and a bottle of Prosecco later, I'm not feeling quite so murderous. In fact I'm beginning to see the possibilities that may have opened up as a result of the Admiral's *letter*.

1. Jason has contacted Freddy. (I'm assuming he bypassed Tory having surmised that the letter had been written by her father).

2. This could well mean that he hasn't in fact shacked up with his bit of stuff, and still actually has feelings for me.

3. He is now aware that other people are aware (is that proper English?) of the fact that Aileen's niece's presence in Bloodstone Tower is most definitely giving the wrong impression to others – namely me...

So, what should I do?

Unfortunately Freddy, who under normal circumstances is second only to the Admiral in the slippery and evasive stakes, has had one too many glasses of wine. So I suggest that we reconvene at my flat tomorrow evening to work out a plan...

Walking back to my flat, I feel happier than I have for some time. I feel sure that it's only a matter of time until Jason is back in my life, the petite redhead is sent packing and I'm working out colour schemes with Tory. ..

It just goes to show how alcohol can affect your brain. Of course I'd forgotten what a complete idiot Jason can be when he's angry.

A sober and contrite Freddy contacted me first thing this morning to say that he'd actually neglected to read right to the bottom of the email Jason had sent him. Apparently he'd panicked after seeing the Admiral's letter and rushed over to meet me without actually reading to the end of Jason's email.

It appears that choosing curtains with Tory is a tad premature. In Jason's words...

'If Kit wanted to get in touch with me, she should have bloody well done it herself instead of asking a lying, cheating interfering meddlesome old bag of wind to do her dirty work.

I have informed Admiral Shackleford that if he ever contacts me again, I will not be responsible for my actions.

Regards

Jason Buchannan

So that's pretty much that then...

~*~

It's the day of little Isaac's Christening and the weather has completely lived up to its promise with not a cloud in the sky. I'm so grateful to Tory for simply allowing me to get on with it. I know she's perfectly capable, but she also knows it's been keeping my mind off the disaster that is my love life.

When I informed her about the fiasco of her father's letter, she was completely mortified. Apparently she'd actively encouraged her father to interfere. It's not often that anyone can lay the blame for the Admiral's cock-ups on someone else, but this was one of those rare occasions.

I couldn't be cross with her though. I know she loves me and just wanted to help. The sight of her wringing her hands in tears quashed any anger I might have had. Nevertheless, when she offered to try and put things right with Jason, I put my foot down. 'He's back to being a complete knob Tory, and quite frankly I don't want anything more to do with him.

'Please don't mention this to your father, I'm sure the put-down that Jason gave him was more than sufficient to prevent him ever going within a hundred miles of Captain Buchannan.'

My voice throughout the whole speech was firm and determined, and if my chin wobbled and my eyes filled with tears, well, neither of us mentioned it.

Anyway, back to the christening. Tory's wearing her favourite navy and white Sophie Loren dress and I've opted for a pale blue halter neck jumpsuit. Little Isaac is sporting a blue sailor suit (what else) and we all blend very aesthetically with my chosen colour scheme...

Before the guests start to arrive, I take a few minutes to stand back and survey the results of all my hard work. A profusion of blue and white bunting surrounds the chairs set up on the lawn. White freesia and deep blue morning glory decorate the makeshift altar and are intertwined through white trellising.

I eye the whole effect critically and frown slightly. Actually it looks a bit like a wedding – I wonder if I might have gone a teensy bit over the top. Maybe I should add some boats and a few teddy bears...

Noah's sister Kim arrived last night with her husband Ben and their two kids. It's the first time they've met Isaac, and Kim hasn't actually let the baby go since she arrived. Of course Tory's more than happy with the additional help, but watching Kim's dreamy, tender expression unaccountably puts my teeth on edge. I suppose I've got used to being the other woman in Isaac's life, and selfishly I don't want him to get too attached to anyone else. I shake my head ruefully – he's not even two months old for goodness sake...

Of course both Freddy and I are Godparents, along with Kim and Ben. There aren't any Hollywood types here this time, it's all very low key – probably due to the potential for disaster in having Boris conduct the service.

The old priest was so pleased to have been asked to do the honours, and since he arrived this morning, Tory's done everything she can to keep him outside and downwind of everybody. I only hope little Isaac doesn't lose his sense of smell as he's brought into the family of God.

The trestle tables have been set up ready for drinks and canapés to be handed round after the service, so unfortunately there's nothing left for me to do. I wonder if it's not the done thing for one of the Godparents to be seen drinking before the ceremony, then I spy Freddy coming through the bi-fold doors carrying two large glasses of bubbly and I decide that of course it's perfectly acceptable.

Heading over to him, I take the full one out of his hand gratefully. 'I assume this is for me,' I mumble through the bubbles. 'Who else?' he responds with shrug and a smile. Grateful for his presence, I look around again at my handy work. 'What do you think?' I ask, expecting my gay friend to rhapsodize over my admittedly enthusiastic decorations. Freddy stares round and opens his mouth to answer...

'Looks like a bloody outdoor brothel.' The Admiral's strident tones get there before him and Freddy looks at my thunderous face with a grin. 'Couldn't have put it better myself.'

Grimacing, I knock back the rest of my Champagne and head over to make a few changes...

In the end, the baptism ceremony was lovely. Whether Boris's nether regions behaved themselves, or the wind was blowing in the right direction, there were no obnoxious odours and the elderly priest's handling of Isaac was a perfect combination of deft and gentle.

Now the religious bit has been dealt with, everybody's starting to relax and there's no better place in the world for a garden party than the Westbrook's back yard. The canapés are delicious and the Champagne is vintage (well at least I think it is – as long as it's cold, it works for me...)

I'm on my third glass and finally beginning to unwind. Looking at my drink, I make a face. Alcohol is the only thing that seems to stop my mind from working overtime at the moment, and I know I can't go on like this. I need to get my life in order.

I glance over to see Flo and Neil being congratulated on their engagement. The whole prospect of becoming a bride has taken years off my aunt. I really am genuinely happy for them both, but seeing them together and so exultant just emphasizes my own stupidity.

Sod sobriety, I'll start again tomorrow. I finish my glass and head over to get another. As I reach the makeshift bar, I glance up towards the house in time to see a figure step through the open bi-fold doors, and freeze. What the bloody hell is Jason doing here?

I have absolutely no idea what to do. My heart is thundering in my chest as though I've run a marathon. Turning quickly back to the bar, I mutely hold out my glass for a refill, all the while mumbling, 'Bugger, bugger, bugger.'

Surely he knew the Admiral would be here? Please, please tell me he's not going to lamp him one. But then he must have known I'd be here too? Is *that* why he's come? Does he want us to be friends? Does he want to tell me he really is shacking up with Aileen's niece? Should I speak first? Should I pretend not to have seen him? Should I simply hide under the bloody table...?

'Hello Kit.' His deep voice over my shoulder makes my knees go weak. I look down to check I haven't spilled anything unsavoury down my front, place my glass down on the table, then turn slowly to face him.

He looks good. In fact he looks completely yummy. The white linen shirt he's wearing highlights his light summer tan. I want to throw myself into his arms crying hysterically, 'I'm sorry...'

'How are you?' is what actually comes out of my mouth, and I congratulate myself that my voice sounds half way normal. He smiles back ruefully and, unbelievably says, 'What do you think?'

I stare at him wordlessly and he steps forward, into my personal space. I stand my ground.

'I'm going to sell Bloodstone Tower,' he murmurs watching me intently. I stare back at him confused, then horrified, and shake my head, whispering, 'No, you can't Jason. What about your father and your grandmother? What about its history? The Tower has belonged in your family since the year dot, it would be so wrong to give it up now.'

'I can't live there without you,' he says simply, 'In fact I don't want to be anywhere without you Kit. If Dartmouth's your home, then it's mine too.'

He raises his hand and rests it on my cheek, whispering, 'I've come down to Dartmouth for that *bit of a chat* you mentioned. You're the only person I've ever wanted to shack up with and I really don't care where we do it.'

I stare at him in stunned silence for a second, then, with a small sob, I give in to temptation and launch myself at him. He catches me and wraps his strong arms tight around my waist, burying his head into my neck, and after a few seconds I realize that I'm not the only one crying. The tears are silently tracking down his cheeks and into my collar. I try to pull back but he won't allow me to, so instead, I lift his face to mine and whisper, 'Please stop my love.' Then I lean forward and place my mouth over his and we kiss like it's the first time ever.

When I finally come up for air, he allows me to step away, still watching me. I realize that he genuinely doesn't know what my answer is going to be. With a small elated smile, I turn back to the bar, take a full bottle of Champagne, together with two glasses, and say, 'We need to go have that chat.'

We escape into a secret arbour situated half way down to the private mooring belonging to the house. There's a two seater swing seat, positioned perfectly to catch the sun as it sets over the river. We sit and for the next few minutes are silent. Then I take his hand and pull it into my lap. Without looking at him, I take a couple of deep breaths, then speak.

'I don't want you to give up your family home Jason.' I feel him tense, ready to interrupt, and I look up, placing my finger over his lips. 'Please, hear me out,' I whisper. 'I don't want you to give up on your dream Jason. I want to share it with you.' I take his hand again and hold it tightly

'It was simply fear that made me back away,' I continue, 'I've always had trust issues. And I've always hated change. Up to now I've made sure that I'm the one to walk away before there's any chance of it all going tits up.' I sigh and lean forward, gripping his hand like a lifeline. 'I thought I was walking away from us for Aunt Flo, but the truth is, I was doing what I always do.

'My aunt doesn't need me. She never did. You were right Jason. And now she has Neil.' I turn to face the man I love with all my heart, still staring at me silently. 'Can we start over Jason? Tell me again that you're retiring from the Navy and you want to convert the pile of rubble that is currently your ancestral home, into a luxury hotel. Ask me to come with you.'

Jason raises my hand to his lips. 'You know I want that more than anything,' he whispers hoarsely, 'But I won't lie to you Kitty Kat, it's going to be tough. Money will be tight – I won't ask Noah for anything more than we actually need.'

And then I remember that he doesn't know anything about my father, so he's not aware that money won't be quite as tight as he imagines.

Feeling as though I've finally come home, I give a joyful smile and tell him…

THE END

Final Author's Note

As I've said in my previous books (I know I'm repeating myself), if you ever find yourself in the South West of England, the beautiful yachting haven of Dartmouth in South Devon is well worth a visit. The pubs and restaurants I describe are real, and I've spent many a happy lunchtime/evening in each of them.

If you'd like more information about Dartmouth and the surrounding areas, you can go to the following website for the Tourist Information Centre:

https://discoverdartmouth.com

In Chasing Victory, I returned to Loch Long in the glorious Scottish Highlands.

If you'd like more information about Loch Long and the magnificent Rosneath Peninsula, please visit the website below:

http://www.trossachs.co.uk/lochs.php

As in Sweet Victory, I have included a list of the Scottish phrases used by Aileen in this book, along with their meanings (just in case you're interested and/or baffled...)

Ah, guid eenin, hou's aw wi ye: Hi, good evening, how are you?

Walcome tae Bloodstone, it's been donkies since a last saw ye: Welcome to Bloodstone, it's been ages since I last saw you.

Noo whaur's that wee bairn: Now where's that baby?

Och ma sweet wean, he's a bonny lad and nae mistake: Oh, the sweet child, he a gorgeous boy and no mistake.

Hou's aw wi ye and that braw man o yours: How are things with you and that handsome man of yours?

Tatties o'wer side and no mistake: It's all gone wrong/disaster's struck.

Keeping in Touch

Thank you so much for reading Chasing Victory, I really hope you enjoyed it.

For any of you who'd like to connect, I'd really love to hear from you. Feel free to contact me via my facebook page at https://www.facebook.com/beverleywattsauthor

If you'd like me to let you know as soon as my next book is available, copy and paste the following link into your browser to sign up to my newsletter and I'll keep you updated about all my latest releases.

https://motivated-teacher-3299.ck.page/143a008c18

And lastly, thanks a million for taking the time to read this story. If you've not yet had your fill of the Admiral's meddling in the Dartmouth Diaries, you might be interested to read my series of cosy mysteries involving the Admiral and Jimmy, aptly titled *The Admiral Shackleford Mysteries*.

Book One: *A Murderous Valentine*, Book Two: *A Murderous Marriage* Book Three: *A Murderous Season* are all available on Amazon.

You might also be interested to learn that the Admiral's Great, Great, Great, Great Grandfather appears in my latest series of lighthearted Regency Romances entitled The Shackleford Sisters.

Book One: *Grace*, Book Two: *Temperance* and Book Three: *Faith* are currently available on Amazon with Book Four: *Hope* to follow soon

Keep reading for a sneak peek of Grace: Book One of The Shackleford Sisters...

Grace

.....Reverend Augustus Shackleford's mission in life (aside from ensuring the collection box was suitably full every Sunday) was to secure advantageous marriages for each of his eight daughters. A tall order, given the fact that in the Reverend's opinion they didn't possess a single ladylike bone in the eight bodies they had between them. Quite where he would find a wealthy titled gentleman bottle headed enough to take any of them on remained a mystery and indeed was likely to test even his legendary resourcefulness.

.....Grievously wounded at the Battle of Trafalgar, Nicholas Sinclair was only recently returned to Blackmore after receiving news of his estranged father's unexpected death. After an absence of twenty years, the new Duke was well aware it was his duty to marry and produce an heir as quickly as possible. However, tormented by recurring nightmares after his horrific experiences during the battle, Nicholas had no taste to brave the ton's marriage mart in search of a docile obedient wife.

.....Never in his wildest dreams did Reverend Shackleford envisage receiving an offer for his eldest daughter from the newly appointed Duke of Blackmore. Of course, the Reverend was well aware he was fudging it a bit in describing Grace as respectful, meek or dutiful, nevertheless, he could never have imagined that his eldest daughter's unruliness might end up ruining them all....

Prologue

The Reverend Augustus Shackleford rested his hands contentedly on his ample stomach and belched loudly, the stew he'd just consumed resting a trifle heavily on his stomach. It was noon at the Red Lion Pub in the village of Blackmore in Devonshire, England, and while he could have quite easily have had his luncheon back at the vicarage, the Reverend much preferred the ale and conversation the pub provided as opposed to the never ending arguing and bickering that came with the unfortunate position of having nine females residing in his house. Though he'd never asked him, the Reverend was content that his dog Freddy was also of the same opinion. The Foxhound was currently curled up under the table happily chasing rabbits in his dreams. Reverend Shackleford was not a man of immense wealth and fortune, and under normal circumstances would be quite content with the fact that the coin in his pocket would more than suffice the cost of the meal he had just consumed.

These were not normal circumstances however and the coin in his pocket – or anywhere else for that matter would certainly not be sufficient to provide the money to set up his only son in the manner befitting a gentleman.

His only son after eight daughters. The Reverend sighed. It had taken three wives to finally produce an heir, but the cost of paying for the eight females he'd been blessed with in the first instance was sorely testing even his creativity – something he'd prided himself on up until now.

He sat morosely staring into his pint of ale next to his long-suffering curate and only friend Percy Noon.

"You know me Percy, I've got a mind as sharp as a well creased cravat, but I've got to admit I'm completely flummoxed as to what to do to raise the coin."

"Perhaps you can find some kind of work for your daughters,

something suitable in polite society for ladies of a gentle disposition," Percy suggested as he pushed his plate aside.

The Reverend snorted. "Have you seen any of my daughters lately?" he scoffed, shaking his head glumly. "Ladies of a gentle disposition? They don't possess a single ladylike bone in the eight bodies they have between 'em. They have no clue how to follow orders or how to comport themselves in any society let alone a polite one.

"If I wish to secure even a modest fortune for Anthony, then I have no recourse but to marry 'em off. Though I can't imagine a man who'd be bacon-brained enough to encumber himself with any of 'em. Unless he was in his cups of course." The Reverend was silent for a while, clearly imagining a scenario where he could take advantage of a well-heeled male whilst the unfortunate victim was suitably foxed. In the end he sighed.

"Percy, the situation is dire indeed. If I don't come up with a plan soon, there's going to be no coin left for Anthony at all. And not only that, we could well find ourselves in the workhouse." He glared at Percy as if it was somehow all his curate's fault. "If that happens Percy my man, there'll be no more bread and butter pudding for you of an evening."

Percy repressed a shudder. He wasn't sure if it was at the prospect of ending up in the workhouse or the thought of Mrs. Tomlinson's bread and butter pudding – the last of which could probably have been used to keep out the drafts. The curate suspected the vicarage cook was a little too fond of Blue Ruin to give much attention to her culinary skills.

"Then your only recourse Sir is to marry them off and marry them well," he stated decisively, settling deeper into his chair. "Somehow."

The Reverend stroked his chin, thinking about his wayward daughters. Each daughter was entirely different than the last. The only similarity they all shared was unruliness. Four of them were already at a marriageable age with the eldest, at twenty-five, a confirmed bluestocking. What chance did he have of marrying any of them off to a gentleman wealthy enough to secure a fortune for his only son?

He was sure that given time he could do it. But it would test even his legendary resourcefulness. Especially if he was going to do it without spending any money.

"Right, we'll need a list of suitable wealthy titled gentlemen bottle-headed enough to take 'em on Percy," he decided, motioning for another mug of ale. "Then we'll let 'em know that I have, err…, good, dutiful daughters who are in need of husbands."

"As you wish Sir," Percy said doubtfully as the serving wench brought another ale for them both. The Reverend picked up his tankard and took a large gulp.

"But before we do that, we'll start by writing down all the positive attributes of the chits so we can emphasize their good points to any prospective husbands. I mean we both know that none of them are exactly bachelor fare, but we can fudge it a bit without anyone being the wiser. At least until they have a ring on their fingers.

"We'll start with Grace since she's the one most likely to end up an old maid if we don't come up with the goods pretty sharpish. Right then Percy, you start."

Silence.

The Reverend frowned. "Thunder an' turf man, surely you can find something good to say about her."

"She has nicely turned ankles," responded Percy a bit desperately.

"Steady on Percy. I certainly hope you've never had an extended opportunity to observe my eldest daughter's ankles otherwise I might have to call you out."

Percy reddened, flustered. "Oh no Sir, not at all, I just happened to notice when she was climbing into the carria…"

"Humph, well I'm not sure we can put that at the top of the list but in Grace's case, we might have to resort to it. I mean why her mother chose to call her Grace is beyond me considering she's distinctly lacking in any attributes remotely divine like. And she's the least graceful person I've ever come across. If there's something to trip over, Grace will find it. Clumsy doesn't even begin to cut it," he added gloomily.

"Well, she has very nice eyes," Percy stated, thinking it best to keep any further observations about the Reverend's daughter above the neck, "And her teeth are sound."

The Reverend nodded, scribbling furiously.

"Can she cook Sir?" The Reverend stopped writing and frowned. "I don't know that she can Percy. At least not in the same capacity as Mrs Tomlinson."

"Probably best not to mention it then," Percy interrupted hastily, unwillingly conjuring up the vision of Mrs. Tomlinson's Bread and Butter pudding again. "And anyway, marriage to a gentleman is not likely to necessitate her venturing into the kitchen." The Reverend nodded thoughtfully.

"How about her voice? Can she sing?"

"Like a strangled cat."

"Dance?"

"I don't think she's ever danced with anyone. I deuced hope not anyway. If she has, I'll have his guts for garters."

"Conversation?" Percy was getting desperate.

"Non existent. I don't think she's spoken more than half a dozen words to me since she was in the crib." The Reverend was becoming increasingly despondent.

"Does she cut a good mother figure to her sisters?"

The Reverend snorted. "I don't think any of 'em are without some kind of scar where she's dropped 'em at some time or another."

"How about her brain?" Percy now resorted to clutching at straws.

"Now that's something the chit has got. Every time I see her, she's got her nose in a book. Problem is, that's the one attribute any well-heeled gentleman will most definitely not be looking for..."

Turn the page for a full list of my books available on Amazon.

Books Available on Amazon

The Dartmouth Diaries:

Book 1 - Claiming Victory
Book 2 - Sweet Victory
Book 3 - All for Victory
Book 4 - Chasing Victory
Book 5 - Late Victory coming soon...

The Admiral Shackleford Mysteries

Book 1 - A Murderous Valentine
Book 2 - A Murderous Marriage
Book 3 - A Murderous Season
Book 4 - A Murderous Paradise coming soon...

The Shackleford Sisters

Book 1 - Grace
Book 2 - Temperance
Book 3 - Faith
Book 4 - Hope coming soon...

Standalone Titles
An Officer and a Gentleman Wanted

About The Author

Beverley Watts

Beverley and her husband live in an apartment overlooking the sea on the beautiful English Riviera.

Between them they have 3 adult children and two gorgeous grandchildren plus a menagerie of animals including 4 dogs - 2 Romanian rescues of indeterminate breed called Florence and Trixie, a neurotic 'Chorkie' named Pepé and a 'Chichon" named Dotty who was the inspiration for Dotty in The Dartmouth Diaries. They also have a cat called Honey.

Beverley spent 8 years teaching English as a Foreign Language to International Military Students in Britannia Royal Naval College which is the premier officer training establishment for the Royal Navy in the UK. She says that in the whole 8 years there was never a dull moment and many of her wonderful experiences at the College were not only memorable but were most definitely 'the stuff of fiction'

An avid reader and writer since childhood, she always determined that on leaving she would write a book. Her debut novel An Officer And A Gentleman Wanted is very loosely based on her adventures at the College.

Beverley has written a series of romantic comedies entitled The

Dartmouth Diaries. Claiming Victory: Book One, Sweet Victory: Book Two, All For Victory: Book Three and Chasing Victory: Book Four, are available on Amazon. Book Five: Late Victory is coming soon...

The first three books of her Admiral Shackleford Cozy Mystery series - A Murderous Valentine, A Murderous Marriage and A Murderous Season - are also available on Amazon. Book Four: A Murderous Paradise is coming soon...

Beverley has now embarked on a new series of Regency Romantic Comedies entitled The Shackleford Sisters. Book One: Grace, Book Two: Temperance and Book Three: Faith are available on Amazon. Book Fouir: Hope is coming soon...

Printed in Great Britain
by Amazon

82336597R00112